Chanekka Pullens Publishing Presents

I0562161

HARRIS II

BY. ROSA JAMES

Contact Information:

Email: misuselsnake@gmail.com

Harris 2 © 2022

Rosa James. All Rights Reserved.

Edited by Chanekka Pullens

Cover Art by PanicAttack/shutterstock.com

ISBN: 979-8-218-09674-8

Printed in the USA

Dedicated to the GRANDS

Naudia

Kah'Loni

Loyal

Adonnis

Riley

TABLE OF CONTENTS

Warning

This book contains fictional events that involve sex, violence, and inappropriate language. Please proceed with caution!!!

CHAPTER ONE

HARRIS

Damn, I cannot believe this shit. My homie and wife-to-be were some snakes. I wonder how long they have been planning this shit. You see, this is a good example on why you cannot trust people because the ones that are in your circle will bite you the hardest. Just think about how most black family history consists of feuding and competition. We are showing our children that it's okay to burn bridges and turn on your family instead of being solid.

"Would you like something to eat?" interrupted a female voice.

Harris turned quickly to find a woman standing in the doorway holding a tray of food. He watched her sashay over to the table and sit the tray down. As she walked back to the door, Harris admired her. She reminded him of Jennifer Lopez. He was so engrossed in watching her from the waist down that he did not notice she was staring dead at him.

"Maybe you can join me on the beach later tonight," said the woman. Harris nodded and turned his focus to the food. The woman smiled and walked away, leaving him to enjoy his meal.

Shit it's already cracking up here. Despite that two people who I considered close to me tried to kill me, you can never pass up an opportunity to have an enjoyable time with a beautiful woman. Besides, I deserve it after what I have been through. But first thing I need to call my people and let them know that I am okay and what happened so they can be on high alert.

Harris noticed a cellphone next to the cup of coffee on the tray. He picked it up and dialed his uncle. The phone rung three times before Bennie answered.

"Hey, Unc, don't look obvious. It's me," whispered Harris.

Bennie sat up from the couch and looked around before responding. "What the hell is going on! We have been looking for you! You took all your money! Did you have to flee? Are the feds on you?"

"All my money? My safe at Twyla's house is empty?" questioned Harris, feeling his stomach turn in knots.

"Hell, yeah, it's empty! That's why I thought you had to flee," responded Bennie, now in the bathroom running the shower.

"Damn, it makes a lot of sense now. Look, you and Rayvin need to get on a plane and come to me. I am in…" Harris paused realizing he had no idea where he was. He placed Bennie on hold and walked out the room to find someone. He walked down the long hallway until he reached the living room where he found the old woman sitting staring out the massive picture window at the ocean.

"Excuse me, ma'am, but where am I? I have some family coming for me," spoke Harris.

The woman turned and offered a warm smile before responding, "We have a hotel in Tampa, Florida. I will have a car take you there so your family can come for you." She handed him a card with the name and address of the hotel.

Harris thanked the woman before returning to Bennie who was still waiting on hold. As he walked back to the bedroom, he read the address to Bennie before ending the call.

I wonder why these people are being so hospitable to me. Don't get me wrong, I am grateful, but things seem too perfect. At this point, I am sure they are not going to harm me because it would have been done or they would have just left me in that shallow grave to die. Harris's thoughts were interrupted by a noise. When he turned, a man was standing in the doorway.

"I know what you are thinking. Why are these people being so nice to you?" spoke the man. He took a couple more steps into the room and continued while jiggling his car keys. "I heard you needed a ride to Tampa."

The man's appearance reminded Harris of the actor *Jorge Ramos*. He nodded while standing up. When the man turned and walked away, Harris grabbed the other breakfast burrito before following.

Once outside the house, Harris took in the warm breeze as he surveyed his surroundings. Everything was beautiful, even the house that he had been staying in.

Damn this beach house looks like some shit off the show *MTV Cribs*. Like I said before, I am grateful for their hospitality. These people are living very well. They own a private airport, a hotel, and this beautiful beach home. I can probably guess what they do for a living, especially if they saved a nigga like me.

Harris noticed the beautiful woman that brought his food standing on the other side of the porch. He remembered the invitation she extended for the beach later.

"I need to take a raincheck on that invite to the beach. But don't worry, I will be back to cash it in."

"I am going to hold you to that," responded the woman, waving goodbye.

Harris laid his eyes on the *1947 Ford Custom Coupe* in the driveway.

"This is nice, everything is original," Harris spoke, getting inside the passenger side.

"Thank you, I don't deal with nothing but authentic things," responded the man, making his way onto the driver's seat.

When the man settled in his seat and started the car, Harris wasted no time asking questions, "So, who are you? You're obviously wealthy, you didn't call the cops when you found and rescued me from a shallow grave."

"If I tell you who I am then I will have to kill you," joked the man, backing out the driveway.

"I get it, but you saved me. So, what's really going on?" quizzed Harris in a more serious tone.

The old man never took his eyes off the road. "I saved you because my wife Carlita insisted. But once I did my research, I realized I needed someone like you. My name is Pax. My wife's older brother Blanca was a part of the cartel before he died. We distribute drugs all over and have been trying to gain a strong presence in the Midwest. That's why you will be a great asset to me."

"I am always down for the hustle so let's discuss business," replied Harris.

"How about we discuss everything after you handle the people that were trying to kill you. I don't want any unnecessary drama interfering with our business," suggested Pax.

"I will get right on that, Pax. Consider that issue resolved." Harris was now staring out the window at the endless water.

A half hour later, Pax parked in front of the lavish hotel.

"Aadi is expecting you. He will be at the front desk. If you need anything or to contact me, just let him know. You can stay in the penthouse for as long as you need under the conditions that we will be doing business together. And remember that this opportunity will not be available for long so handle your issue quick."

Harris got out the car and went inside the hotel, then Pax drove away. As he walked through the lobby, people gave looks of disgust at his dirt covered clothing. He figured he probably looked homeless and hoped to find Aadi soon so he could get to a room and wash his clothing.

Well, this is awkward, my first time feeling embarrassed in years. I remember the first time I ever experienced embarrassment. I was ten and my mother was walking around the projects begging the dealers for a high. My uncle and aunt were not around at the time, so I tried to handle things. But that was a bad idea. She jerked away from me and began yelling, cursing me out. Cameron was there. He told me it was going to be okay, and we walked away.

I can't believe he turned into a Loyal Snake. It's amazing how people can go through so much with you and over time develop a hate for your happiness and success. But I have him and Twyla to thank for this scenario I am in now. Just think if they didn't try to kill me, then Pax and Carlita would have never had to save me. Now I am about to take my hustle to a whole other level. Not to sound arrogant, but the fact is you can't kill a Scarface nigga like me.

Harris walked through the lobby to the front desk. When he spotted the only man behind the counter, he gave him a nod. Aadi returned the nod and led Harris to the elevator and up to the penthouse. He gave him a private cell before giving him his privacy.

Now alone, Harris walked around admiring how luxurious things were. He dialed his uncle again who answered on the first ring.

"Rayvin and I are on the way to the airport to get on our flight now. We will see you in about three hours," said Bennie before hanging up.

While waiting, Harris showered. The penthouse was equipped with a small washer and dryer, so he washed his dirt soiled clothing. He made sure to tell Aadi that he was expecting his family before laying on the couch and falling asleep.

Hours later he was awakened by Rayvin and Bennie standing over him.

"Look at this nigga all naked and shit like a newborn fresh out the pussy," joked Bennie.

Harris sat up on the couch and yawned.

"So, what the hell is going on?" questioned Rayvin, admiring Harris's package.

Harris retrieved his clothing from the dryer and dressed before spending the next hour explaining what happened. When he told them that Cameron and Twyla were involved in his disappearance, Rayvin was furious and ready to fly back to Kansas City and kill them both.

"Rayvin, I need to handle this myself, my way," insisted Harris.

"Man, I knew that nigga Cameron was shady ever since you two were kids," said Bennie, lighting up his cigar.

"I want to get that bitch Twyla! Ever since she came into the picture things have been fucked up," said Rayvin, pacing the floor.

"Calm down, Rayvin, I will deal with Twyla the way I need to. I know it's all fucked up but look at where it got us. Try and focus on that," said Harris.

I know they don't want to hear this but honestly, I feel bad for Twyla. I can understand why she came for me. I just want to give her a pass. I will not trip about the money because there is not enough money to compensate for her mother's life. If she stays in her lane, I will stay in mines.

"Look, we are not going to kill Twyla because she was only doing what we all would have done. If she stays in her lane, we can move on and focus on this money," said Harris.

He sat back and prepared himself for the reactions from both Bennie and Rayvin.

As predicted, Rayvin stopped pacing and looked at Bennie who sat comfortable on the couch still enjoying his cigar.

Before she could say a word, Harris interrupted her, "Look, Rayvin, I need you to trust me on this. I am the reason why she grew up without a mother."

Rayvin turned her focus to the beautiful view. She wanted to trust Harris but craved retribution. Bennie continued to sit in silence. He wanted blood but was more interested in the business opportunity that his nephew mentioned.

"So just to clarify, we need to cut our grass before proceeding to this bag?" Bennie questioned.

"That's right. We will go back to Kansas City, I will handle this nigga Cameron, and come back here to get things rolling," responded Harris.

"We will get eyes on him; I am sure that's what Rayvin is texting in her cell over there. We will go handle this shit and move forward to better things. But I think you being MIA works in our advantage right now. It creates a great scenario to why Cameron turns up dead. Make sure you are not seen by anyone. We will plant some seeds and people will assume that you two rubbed someone the wrong way and caught karma behind it," said Bennie.

"I agree, but I need my kids," responded Harris, now feeling sad.

"No worries, just lay low for a minute and I promise you will see your children soon. By the way, this seems like a wonderful place to relocate. I can see Effie and Lil Ben chilling down here!" finished Bennie.

Rayvin cell phone rung. When she answered, it was her homie in Kansas City with the information she needed.

"Okay, we have eyes on Cameron. Can you believe he is rolling around the city like nothing has happened. I also planted a rumor that you and Cameron got into some shit with some major people that want you two dead. So, let's get the flights and go handle his ass," said Rayvin.

"Good move, little hitter!" proclaimed Bennie.

"We not flying commercial, the people that own this hotel also own a private airport. I will call Aadi and get shit arranged," said Harris, grabbing his cell and calling Aadi.

After talking to Aadi, Harris ordered dinner, and everyone spent the rest of the night relaxing before falling asleep. Hours later, Harris was awakened by the younger woman from the beach house. His dick was already at attention as he continued to lay in the bed allowing the woman to slip his boxers off. She climbed onto his erection and began riding him with precision causing him to release low moans. Harris clinched his teeth while gripping her hips. He was trying to hold on and not cum too fast, but in less than five minutes, he released.

"Damn, no one has made me cum so quick," Harris said to himself.

The woman gave him a kiss on the lips before standing up from the bed.

Harris watched her slip into her dress. There was no point in questioning how she got inside the penthouse because they owned the place.

"My name is Abriella, Pax and Carlita are my uncle and aunt," responded Abriella.

Harris looked over at the mirror before cradling his head. He was already crashing the plane before it took off.

Damn, I fucked Pax niece! This could fuck up our business relationship that has not even started yet. For the real hustlers out there if you can help it, keep your dick out of your business. This can only end in two ways, 1) Pax will have me killed or 2) I will have to marry this bitch.

Harris slipped into his boxers and sat back onto the edge of the bed. He was now gloating because he may have made things complicated by Abriella.

"You look worried, is everything okay? Was my conito good?" questioned Abriella.

"Oh, that pussy was right, just how I imagined it. But what we just did could mess up the business I was trying to establish with your uncle," replied Harris.

Abriella laughed before responding, "Don't worry about that! I am the business! My uncle sent me here. He already knew I was into you. Believe me, you will be seeing a lot of me. A car will be waiting at 9:00am to take you three to the private airport. When you return, you will have to fly commercial. Just come back to the hotel and Aadi will let us know you are back for business. Don't keep me waiting."

Harris walked Abriella to the door and gave her a long passionate kiss before closing it. When he turned around Rayvin was standing with her arms folded.

"I see almost dying has not changed your taste for pussy," she spoke, shaking her head.

Harris shrugged and headed to the kitchenette to grab a bottled water. He knew Rayvin was right but it was too late so he could only hope it did not sabotage his new business opportunity.

CHAPTER TWO

CAMERON

I know you think that I am a piece of shit. Harris and I were like brothers, but his problem has always been these bitches. He caused my woman Twyla grief being the cause of her mother committing suicide along with not giving me what I deserved. I was tired of watching him live the good life while I struggled taking care of my four brothers, three sisters, parents, and grandparents.

My family and I lived in the projects just like Bennie and Harris. My parents worked hard but it was always a constant struggle, especially taking care of eight children. My grandparents had social security income, but their medical expenses ate most of that.

The difference between my family and Harris's was that my family had morals and values, while his family were straight gangsters. My parents tried to stay hopeful through all the struggle, but fact was they had failed. I heard the story of my father being the one that was supposed to make it out the ghetto. He had skills in basketball, but I never saw him play. He and my mother were high school sweethearts. My mother was a nurse. But like most families in the eighties, crack cocaine was the downfall.

When I as very young, I remember we lived in a big house in a subdivision. My parents had nice cars, we took vacations, but that was short lived once my father's addiction took over. My mother struggled to maintain, then she lost her medical license because my father was stealing from the doctor's office she worked at. Instead of snitching her husband out and saving her family, my dedicated ass mother took the fall. I swear love will have you on bullshit. I think at the end of the day their marriage was more important than anything, even their own children's wellbeing. No matter what was happening, they always continued to pride themselves on being married.

Harris used to look out for me when we were adolescents, giving me his gently used shoes and clothing. Once we were old enough, Bennie put us on. At the beginning, I was content with making enough money for my siblings to have the latest shoes and clothes so they would not be teased. When the food stamps ran out, I was able to buy groceries, so our dinners were more lavish than before. For a few years, things were better, and I started to stack money. Then the grounds manager of the complex found out I was hustling, and an eviction notice came shortly after.

My family had three months to move, and we no longer qualified for public housing with drug trafficking on our record. We needed to buy a house, so I hustled harder to stack the money. Meanwhile, Harris and his family had moved out the projects and were living well. He had options and didn't have to do anything but push weight. But he was greedy and continued to sale pieces in the projects.

Bennie was investing his money and preparing to go more legit. He was linking up with businesses across the city, buying properties to flip and rent. The only thing he maintained in the streets was the connect that no one had. Every move he made he included Harris, and I began to envy that. I knew Bennie did not like me and when I mentioned it to Harris, he acted oblivious, explaining that Bennie was just hardcore and did not know how to express love.

Me and him both knew that was not the case by the shitty eight balls Bennie was giving me. The night Bennie and I killed Rayvin's brothers was the only time he seemed to be cool with me. But now that I think back it was probably because he was setting me up to take the fall if needed.

I learned later that I was not the only one that noticed that Bennie treated me differently. One night I was out on the wall hustling as usual. The OG Dorsey approached me, and we began talking. You see, Dorsey was what hustlers didn't want to end up being. He was over fifty years old, still living in public housing, a broke acholic, on child support, had different baby mommas scattered around the projects, stayed in jail for domestic violence, was cheap, and had one decked out car that was the only reminder that he had money years ago.

Dorsey questioned the validity of my brotherhood with Harris. He said that if we were family, then why was I still struggling. His words played in my head as I continued to hustle. When I turned in for the night, I counted my money, realizing that he was right. Why was Harris not breaking bread with me like I would have if I had it.

I know what you are thinking, why not just ask him for the help. Well to be honest, it was my pride, and the nigga was not blind. He was seeing the struggle firsthand he just ignored it. If someone from the outside looking in could see it, then I was sure everyone else did. With that realization, I felt like everyone was looking at me like I was stupid. Fact was that Harris and Bennie was just letting me live around them and not trying to uplift me like brothers are supposed to do.

But despite my feelings, I needed them for the drug supply because the clock was ticking. My family and I would be out in a matter of weeks. By the end of that summer, I raised the money just in time for the sheriff to come knocking to enforce the notice to vacate. I remember seeing Dorsey chilling as usual when I parked the moving truck in front of the house. He yelled across the parking lot, "that shit should not be happening to you, little homie!"

I didn't bother to respond as I watched my family scrambled to grab their belongings. The sheriff did not care that it started raining as he sat inside his truck watching us. That night we only grabbed our necessities and what we held dear to us which was not much. It was a sad and an embarrassing experience but there was light at the end of the tunnel.

I was able to find a house in one of my mother's favorite areas, *Manheim Park*. The ten-bedroom, three full bathroom home was a perfect fit for my large family. There was an elementary, middle, and high school in walking distance, and a park to play that was not contaminated with drug dealers and addicts. I got the house for dirt cheap because it needed a lot of work, and the family was just trying to get rid of it.

When I turned the key and opened the door, the look on my families' faces were priceless and worth the late-night hustling. That night I felt like I could do anything, and I vowed to make sure my family was never homeless again.

Now like I said before the house needed major work. A new roof, furnace, some paint, and windows. My father and I made the house livable for the winter and continued to do any work that we could to avoid having to pay others.

My parents didn't agree with me in the drug game, but life had humbled them, so they stop bothering me about my lifestyle and just prayed that I made it home every night.

Seeing my family happy had me content again but I had to stay on top. The house was a money pit for the first couple of years. Harris and his uncle had people that could do the work for a little bit of nothing, but they had them so tied up in their projects, I could not get any cheap help. But I prevailed and was able to start saving money again. But this only lasted for a little while because my grandmother died. With no life insurance, I had to pay for everything in cash. This left me with only $5,000 in my stash and that would be gone soon because I had to pay the bills and keep food in the house.

Then one of my younger sisters got pregnant with twins so now we had two new mouths to feed. Man, I was barely staying afloat trying to take care of home and keep up with the lavish lifestyle that Harris lived. He and his uncle were working and playing hard. It was nothing for them to hit the club every other day making it rain, buying bottles for bitches.

I had to stay in the scene with them because Harris was a brand. Just being affiliated with him had its benefits. When it was all said and done, I was living in the shadows. At that point, I was no longer going home at night and just hustling around the clock, crashing at any project bitch crib that would let me in. I ran into Dorsey often and he kept saying the same thing. I finally decided to question why he was so invested in my situation with Harris. At this point, it had to be a motive, or he was just being a full-time hater.

Dorsey told me that he had been around the hood for a long time and seen a lot of things. That was not surprising to me. He claimed to know the real reason I was being treated bad by

Bennie. He would not go into detail. However, he advised me to confront Bennie and if he was a real nigga, he would tell me the truth. He left me with only a hint that the information was life changing and he knew Harris knew nothing about it.

Days later, I remember meeting with Bennie at a Mexican restaurant on the west side of town. When I arrived, Bennie was already at the bar having a drink and chatting with the owner. I took a seat and ordered a shot before getting to the point.

My exact words were, "Bennie, why are you starving me out here? What did I ever do to you?"

He laughed at my poor choice in words as he ordered another round of shots. But I also noticed the disgust in his eyes. Being who he was, Dorsey was right, he would not lie about how he felt about me.

"Check this out, I don't give two fucks about you, Cameron, and the only reason why I even do the small business with you is because you and Harris are so close," spoke Bennie, never breaking his cold stare.

His look and those words were all I needed to confirm he hated me. I was on my own out here and had to figure out how to level up. During that conversation, I made one mistake by mentioning Dorsey's name and that mistake would be costly for him. When I went to the hood the next day, word around was that Dorsey was dead. From that point on, I knew to keep my distance from Bennie because he was dangerous and would simply kill someone for mentioning his name.

While I continued to find my way, Harris continued to move up. Just like his uncle, he was buying properties, investing more, and never offered me anything. So, I just continued to keep my head down and hustle until an opportunity presented itself.

Eventually, an opportunity came when Harris fucked Cookie's head up. She started doing drugs. I was able to set up shop in her place. I found Dorsey's plug and was able to get my own drugs. But I made the mistake of staying in the same place to sale. Niggas started coping from me and when Bennie found out, the connect disappeared. Once again, I was right back under Bennie's umbrella, and he was being even more shitty with the drugs he gave me.

One night he paid me a visit at Cookie's place. He told me this was his city and if I wanted to be the top dog, then I needed to move to another state. I was not ready to move to another state and I could not go to another hood because I had rivals everywhere by being affiliated with Harris. So, I continued to hustle and make money while keeping an eye on Twyla.

Things started looking up again, then my mother got sick. My father relapsed and started doing crack and we had to kick him out for trying to sale everything that was not nailed down.

Feeling overwhelmed, I sent the five youngest siblings and my grandfather down south to stay with family. The two oldest stayed in Kansas City, got jobs, went to school, and helped to take care of our mother. The Medicaid would not pay for all the medications, so I had to pay out of pocket. It was like my stash would never grow and I started to think God was telling me something like, "get a fucking job."

I didn't listen to the signs and continued my role with Harris. But now only changing the fact that I was conspiring to take what was his. I had to be careful around Bennie because it was like he had a six sense. I would be lying if I say that I was not afraid of that man along with a lot of niggas in the city.

But my fear of Bennie did not stop me from becoming Harris's biggest hater. Yeah, I turned into a *Loyal Snake.*

I continued to hustle at Cookie's. That was the only place I could control because Harris did not want to be there. Then she committed suicide. Feeling defeated, I just enrolled in college and started filling out job applications.

Harris was so far in the clouds he had no idea that I was working an actual job as a security guard at a nursing home while taking classes at the local community college. I was doing my elective classes until I decided what I wanted to do, and the financial aid was keeping a nigga out the dark. But we were suffering, and the stress was taking a toll on me.

I had no other choice but to sale the big house and use the money to relocate my family down south. I was done with Kansas City and ready to get on the right path and enjoy life. Twyla had also moved from Kansas City. She was going to nursing school and I would travel to see her quite often.

When she graduated from nursing school, we were in the middle of figuring out where we wanted to live so we could start a family. But something happened on the five-year anniversary of Cookie's death when Twyla went back to Kansas City to visit her gravesite. She ran into Harris at a store. He approached her flirting not realizing who she was.

That set her off and she wanted blood. I told her to leave it alone and just move on, but she was not so I had to get involved again. I returned to Kansas City and started getting drugs from Bennie again and getting back into the flow of things with Harris. While I was doing that, Twyla was conspiring the master plan that would end with Harris dead and our pockets fat.

It took her a lot of convincing to make me go along with her being boo'd up with Harris. But she got right in and swept that nigga off his feet. It was hilarious and agonizing at the same time. Twyla used to have to talk me down every day from blowing the whistle. The closer they got to the wedding, the more I became anxious. Twyla seemed to be procrastinating and their chemistry was amazing. It was her idea to do the marriage thing. Deep down, I felt like once she got married that the tables were going to turn on me, so I started pressing for us to make the move. When she found out the combination to the safe, it was time.

After we buried Harris, I cleaned out the safe before Bennie came for it. I was nervous the next few days because like I said before, Bennie was a beast. He was like lucifer, and Rayvin was not far behind him. I had Twyla take the money and go find us a place in Texas. The plan was for her to find a house, a job as a nurse and once I came, we would live happily ever after. I am only sticking around in Kansas City so I won't look suspicious. Everything is going to be set up in Texas. I used some of the money from the safe and purchased a family house in Houston for my mom, grandfather, and siblings. I brought some commercial property that I will rent to business owners, and we are starting a family business, a food catering company. It will be called Home Again Catering because the women in our family can burn in the kitchen.

Cameron lit his blunt and relaxed in the recliner. He could not wait for Twyla to find a place so he could leave. He was feeling good because he finally won and once he left Kansas City, there would be no turning back. He pressed play on his cell and began listening to Anita Baker. Suddenly, Harris crept out of the darkness. When Cameron opened his eyes, he was staring down the barrel of a gun.

"So, you finally made it," said Harris before pulling the trigger.

He shot Cameron in the chest twice, once in the face, and one in the head before leaving out the backdoor. On the next block, Rayvin and Bennie waited. Harris changed clothing while riding in the back seat to the airport. He would go back to Florida and start his new business endeavor with Pax.

CHAPTER THREE
RETRIBUTION

Now I know that you did not soak up that bullshit Cameron was spitting. This nigga blamed me for his struggle. Fuck that! He had the same hustling opportunities as I. And that shit about my uncle? Maybe he saw the snake in him from the beginning.

It is not my job to fix his life. Just like my family was out here hustling hard, he and his family should have been on the same shit. My family were wolves and Cameron was the sheep in wolf clothing. If I were him, I would have figured out a way to get mines. But to think he was going to get at me. He should have just pumped me with bullets and left me dead in the streets we ran in. To think I really thought highly of him when he was a Loyal Snake. He let a bitch do the thinking for him. Just think if he would have just simply shot me dead. No one would have suspected him of committing the crime because I have so many haters.

That's what he gets for trying to overthink with his bitch, now he is rotting, waiting for someone to discover his body. If I give you any advice, I recommend that you stay in your lane and never think another person is responsible for helping you.

Cameron wanted to be equal, but I would always be two steps ahead because our family's foundation was solid. Our business started with my grandfather and was passed to my mother, Aunt Rachel and Uncle Bennie who then pulled me into the game. I imagine that my grandfather and Cameron was in the same situation. They were the sole bread winners and had to pull their families up.

My grandfather died trying and our family was still in the hood. So, my aunt, mom and uncle took over and hustled hard. And just like Cameron's father, my mother struggled with drug addiction. My aunt went to prison only to serve her time and get murdered a short time after being released.

One of Cameron's errors was that he was a follower that wanted to received leader benefits. If he were smart, he would have pulled his brothers into the game and schooled them. He was given the resources and failed which clearly means he was not built for this. Fact is, you fight your way to the top and don't expect anyone to give you handouts. Cameron spent a lot of his time sizing me and my family up instead of strategizing on how to get his and I am going to leave it at that.

Now that Cameron was dead it was time to go back to Tampa and get the money. Now on the private plane, Harris relaxed and stared out the window admiring the clouds. But his idle mind made him continue to think about Cameron. He thought about some of the good times they had. He searched his memory trying to see if there were any warnings that it would come to this.

A couple hours later, he landed at the private airport where Aadi was waiting. When Aadi observed his attire, he twisted his face. Harris noticed the look and addressed it once he entered the car.

"Look, when in the trenches appearance is usually the last thing on your mind," said Harris.

"Very true, but once you're over the clouds, appearance is everything for many reasons," replied Aadi.

Harris looked over and nodded in agreement before instructing Aadi to take him to the nearest mall to purchased clothing. Once again, Aadi frowned because bosses did not shop at malls. A half hour later Aadi parked in front of Greiner's Fine Men Clothing Store.

They went inside and Harris purchased two suits along with a few Polo shirts, slacks, shoes, underwear, and other accessories. Before leaving, Harris dressed in a white linen shirt, jeans, and white G/FORE leather sneakers.

When he exited the dressing area, Aadi nodded and spoke, "Guess you decided to save the suit for later, but you're off to a good start."

"I know the deal, Aadi," responded Harris as they exited the store.

They went to the hotel where Pax, Carlita, and Abriella awaited.

"So now that you have handled your issues in Kansas City, let's get to the business," said Pax.

From that point, Abriella began to explain everything. Harris would become the major distributor for the southeast region along with the Midwest. He would have shares of a new dispensary in Colorado.

"You see, we want all money, but we prefer it clean as possible. So, we take the dirty money and clean it in lucrative businesses across the country like hotels, casinos, dispensaries once they get off the ground, even certain produce," said Abriella.

"Well, my uncle already distributes drugs in the Midwest," said Harris.

"But we are talking about replacing the person he gets his shit from, the middleman," said Pax.

"So, what are the percentages on the businesses?" questioned Harris, still feeling like a house nigga.

The offer was giving him more clean money, but he still felt like he was going to be only a manager instead of the head nigga in charge.

"We get the drugs from the cartel so it's cheaper. The clean business opportunities are discussed among the group and we usually all split the investment. However, when your money long enough, you are welcome to grab your own as well.

Trust me, in the blue-collar world things seem to run better when you have a team of people with money," responded Carlita.

"Okay, well, you have a deal. I am sure my uncle would agree with the numbers," Harris lied, knowing that Bennie would never drop his connect.

"Perfect. We will be in touch in a few days to get things going. And may I give you some advice. Don't shit where you lay your head," said Pax before leaving.

"I look forward to doing business with you," said Carlita, patting Harris on the back. She caught up with her husband who was in the hall waiting by the employee elevator.

Finally alone, Abriella did not waste any time crawling across the marble conference table until she was in front of Harris. She opened her legs, revealing her freshly Brazilian waxed pussy.

"Are you ready for dinner," she whispered in a seductive voice before releasing her DD breasts.

Without hesitation, Harris dove face first into Abriella's love box, savoring all her juices.

"Oh, my God. Yes, keep your tongue right there," whispered Abriella.

As he continued to ravish her, Harris could not help but to think that Abriella was going to get him in trouble.

One Week Later

Twyla returned to find Cameron's decomposing body in his reclining chair. She muffled her screams as she paced the floor. Instead of calling the authorities, she collected her mother's items and left. She knew Bennie or Rayvin was responsible for his death and did not want to risk staying in Kansas City any longer. She cried as she drove for hours down south trying to get far away from Kansas City.

She tried to imagine the life Cameron wanted for them. He wanted to build or buy a home in Houston, Texas and have a couple of children.

The thoughts of children reminded Twyla of the positive pregnancy test she tossed into the trash at the airport. She knew it was Harris's baby because she missed a couple birth control pills. Her plan was to return, have sex with Cameron, and convince him the baby belonged to him. But now he was dead, and she was alone.

CHAPTER FOUR
BENNIE

I know it sounds treacherous, but I am glad that Cameron is dead. From the day he was born, I knew that he would be a problem because of his father Kevin. You see, out of respect for my sister Cassandra, no one knew that Kevin is also my nephew's father.

Before Harris was born, Cassandra and Kevin were having a secret affair behind his girlfriend Melba's back. When Cassandra found out she was pregnant, she kept it a secret from everyone. I found out about it when our parents were out of town, and she went into labor.

I remember finding her on the bathroom floor, holding her stomach while crying out in pain. My other sister Rachel who was twenty-one at the time, took us to the hospital. For a teenage boy, the experience of childbirth was both traumatizing and amazing. To be in the room while a baby is born creates an attachment that can never be broken. But all that blood, yelling, and pain are many of the reasons why I didn't get anyone pregnant until I was much older to handle that.

After Harris was born, we all stayed at the hospital until Cassandra was discharged. Our parents were due back home in another week. Rachel and I used the emergency money to buy baby supplies along with essentials for Cassandra. I helped my sister take care of her baby; I remember sleeping on the floor in her bedroom. When Harris woke up, we both took care of him.

A couple days before our parents returned, I was awakened by a commotion. I checked on Harris, who was still sleeping, before going to see what was going on. When I made it to the top of the stairs, I overheard Rachel and Cassandra arguing with a man.

As I continued to listen, it was Kevin. He was denying Harris being his son. Cassandra yelled obscene words while Rachel made threats to make his life a living hell. I heard a scuffle, so I rushed downstairs in time to witness Cassandra on the floor and Rachel pointing a gun at Kevin. He held his hands up while backing out the front door. That night Cassandra cried a river while I took care of Harris.

When our parents returned, I sat outside on the front stairs and listened to my family arguing inside. Cassandra would not tell who the father was. My father began beating Cassandra demanding her to tell him. My mother tried to stop him because he was getting out of control. Not able to take it, Rachel told him. My father stopped as soon as he heard Kevin's name and barged out the front door. He headed to the bottom of the complex to confront him. I followed him but kept a distance just in case bullets started flying.

I made it around the building in time to witness my father knock Kevin the fuck out. My father waited for him to wake up before telling him he had a son to take care of. He emptied Kevin's pockets and left him still sitting on the sidewalk.

Even though Kevin was afraid of my father and embarrassed, he still picked himself up from the ground and yelled that Harris was not his son. My father came back around the building, but my mother caught him just in time before he pulled his gun.

Once my parents were out of sight, Kevin and his friends laughed about the situation. I stood watching him take my nephew and sister as a fucking joke, and I knew at that point I would make him suffer for denying them.

Then months later, I found out that the reason why Kevin was not claiming Harris was because he had a son on the way with his girlfriend. Melba and Kevin were an item and Cassandra was the dark secret. The cute couple had a lot going for themselves and was destined to get out the hood. Kevin played basketball and Melba was the honor student with college offers from all over the country. When she became pregnant, her parents planned to keep the baby while she pursued her dreams.

My mother tried talking to Kevin's parents, but they were convinced that Harris was not their son's baby. Angry, my father started pressing Kevin every day until his family picked up and moved out the projects. However, the tension didn't stop him from sneaking back to the projects against his family's advice. I would always see him and could have told my father or had his goons get on him, but the revenge would be mines and a bullet would not be enough.

My father gave me good advice but was not following it in this situation. His exact words were, "the best retribution is simmered slow to perfection."

While I waited for my simmering pot of retribution, Cassandra fell into a deep depression. She tried to function and keep a straight face. But to cope, she began doing drugs and neglecting Harris. Me, my parents, and Rachel took care of him. Then my homie told me that he saw Kevin picking Cassandra up on several late nights. When I confronted her, she snapped and told me to stay out of her business. Things took a turn for the worst when my father was shot to death while sitting inside his car one night. During that time, I was sixteen years old.

I had to step into my father's shoes and stay on top. I went from straight A's in school to staying up late nights out on the grit.

One night Rachel and I were outside hustling because it was the first of the month when this nigga Kevin had to nerve to approach us. He must have thought we were soft now that our father was gone. He began talking to us like we were cool. We learned that he received a basketball scholarship that would pay for his full ride in college.

Rachel was ready to put a bullet in his knees, but I told her to stand down because she was a hot head like our father.

Tonight, I was going to hear Kevin out. Maybe he was going to step up and be a father to Harris.

He continued talking about how he did not want to lose his relationship with Melba. She told him that if she ever found out that Harris was really his son, she would leave him and never let him see Cameron again. I was disappointed that he was letting a bitch get in the way. He must have seen the disappointment in my eyes because he tried to apologize but to his misfortune his words were now falling upon deaf ears.

We all sat in silence for several seconds before Kevin started begging for weed. Remember that pot of retribution that was simmering? It was time to cash it in. I jumped off the wall and retrieved the bag of weed from my pocket. I turned my back and rolled three blunts and one was laced with crack. I turned to Kevin and handed it to him and said, "It's all good, player, just send my nephew some of that basketball money when you start making it."

We all lit our personal blunts. Rachel and I sat and smoked while watching Kevin puff his Primo. In between drags, he continued to brag about college. After that night months went by, and we did not see Kevin at all. Then one night I saw him walking around and it was clear he was jonesing.

He approached me and asked if I had some crack. I smiled and handed him an 8-ball and said don't smoke it all in one place. He nodded before hurrying away. I did not see him again for a few years. But word around the hood was that Kevin was kicked out of college and was in and out of rehab. I was satisfied that I sabotaged his future. Cassandra was in and out of rehab, but she was fighting hard to win the war against addiction.

Life went on. We no longer worried about whether Kevin was going to be in Harris's life because he was not even capable of shaking his nasty crack habit. My sister continued to struggle but we would stand strong with her journey.

Then my mother became gravely ill. On the night she died, before taking her last breath she pleaded with Cassandra to get clean. My sister agreed to go, and we took her following my mother's funeral service. We made sure it was far away from Kevin. We found a good rehab in California. It was costly but that just made us hustle harder. Being young adults with no parents and a kid, our lives were on the line.

Now it was just me, Rachel, and Harris. The complex manager let us stay because she was good friends with our parents. Being the man of the house, I had to hustle harder and do whatever it took to get money.

You see, it's a different beast when you have people depending on you. I had to do a lot of fucked up shit to people to keep my family straight. In the streets, anything goes when trying to survive. My happiness is watching my people eat and live carefree. And yeah, I sold my soul, especially when I gave my first piece of crack to a junkie. And I validated it when I gave Kevin that crack knowing it was going to ruin his life. I can't help it; I am a beast.

But back to Kevin, time passed and before I knew it, he and his wife Melba moved back to the projects with their mini basketball team. Kevin walked around talking about he was saved and that his kids were going to be successful and get out the hood. That's one of the reasons why I pulled Cameron into hustling, to spite his father.

While Cameron was watching my nephew's pockets get fatter, I was making sure he never prospered under my umbrella.

When he confronted me about why I hated him, I did not hide my feelings, but I did not tell him the whole truth either. When he mentioned Dorsey, I found him that same night and killed him.

And now Cameron is dead, my mission is complete. It's time to make some changes. I have been living in Kansas City, Missouri all my life. So maybe it's time to leave here.

Bennie continued to relax on his deck while smoking a blunt and enjoying a glass of whiskey. Inside, Effie and Lil Ben were asleep on the couch after watching The Lion King.

Suddenly, Effie was awakened by a knock on the front door. She took her time standing to stretch before going to the door and looking through the peephole. When she saw Loretta, she checked the clock and frowned because it was after midnight.

She opened the door. "It's late, Loretta, is everything okay? You usually call before you come."

"I just need to talk, and you were the only person I could think of," responded Loretta.

Effie stood to the side, allowing her to enter. As she walked inside, Effie noticed the beads of sweat on her forehead and she was not dressed in her usual glam girl attire.

"Can I get you something to drink?" asked Effie, closing the front door.

"No, thank you, I just need to talk," responded Loretta.

Effie took a seat on the couch next to Lil Ben. She watched Loretta who seemed fidgety for several seconds.

"You're not doing that coke again are you, Loretta? You seem really antsy," questioned Effie.

Loretta checked her surroundings before she responded, "I was thinking back when we were in school, and you were in the bathroom getting beat by Shantae and her crew and I saved you?"

Effie rolled her eyes; she knew that whenever Loretta mentioned the bathroom incident, she either had an issue or was going to ask a big favor.

"You know I remember! I was the one getting my ass beat. So, tell me what's really going on. You don't seem yourself."

"You are not a real friend, and I should have never helped you," said Loretta, now pointing a gun.

Effie's eyes widened as she placed her arms up. "Loretta, what the fuck are you doing? Put the gun down."

"No! I helped you and we have always had everything together. Then when you get with this nigga Bennie, you change and stop having my back. You did not tell me about Harris giving my daughter to that bitch Tameka. In fact, you act like you don't know me anymore," spat Loretta.

"Loretta, you are high and tripping. After Harris and you fell out, you started punishing me like it was my fault. I tried to be there for you, but you have to want to help yourself," said Effie.

"Bitch, you were my friend! And you up here chilling with the people that took my daughter."

"Loretta, you are tripping! Now let's be honest, you did not want Karris if her father didn't want you. You are so sad, a miserable gold digger," spat Effie.

"So, you saying I wasn't worth it? That I did not deserve to be a mother or wife?" inquired Loretta, now standing up and securing the gun in her hands preparing to shoot.

"Hey, what the fuck is going on in here," interrupted Bennie, entering the living room.

Startled, Loretta fired the gun three times shooting Bennie.

"Oh, my God, no! Why are you doing this," yelled Effie as she grabbed her son and hurried over to Bennie who laid on the floor not moving.

Loretta dropped the gun and hurried out the house not looking back. She ran down the block, hopped inside her car, and sped away.

CHAPTER FIVE
LORETTA

I hope that Bennie is dead. With him and Harris gone, the rest of the family will crumble.

I can't help but to think that Effie was right when she said I did not want Karris. But she is mines and it's the principle of it all. I refuse to allow Harris and his family to just throw me away like trash because I don't meet their standards.

My breaking point started when Harris came up missing and I went to jail for busting out May's car windows. While I was locked up, Effie put money on my books and showed up to my court date instead of bailing me out. When I was finally bailed out three weeks later, it was Cameron waiting at the gate to pick me up. He opened the passenger door, and I hopped inside the car. I put on my seat belt while he walked around to the driver side and got in.

We drove in silence for several minutes before he asked me if I wanted something to eat. I nodded and he drove to a Popeye's Chicken. We went inside to order our food and sat. We ate in silence for several minutes before Cameron began to speak again. He told me that Harris was dead and that he always felt sorry for how everyone treated me.

When I tell you those words meant so much to me. I never paid Cameron any attention because he was not the one with the money. Now he was driving a BMW and had posted my bail. He was the man now and maybe he bailed me out for more reasons than just feeling sorry for me.

After eating, he took me shopping and money was not a thing. He was patient as he watched me shop until I dropped. Next, he took me to the Marriott hotel downtown and paid for me a room for a week. This was the treatment I wanted from Harris but since he was dead it didn't matter anymore. Before Cameron left, he gave me $2,000 and told me he would return in a couple days to check on me. That meant I had a day to get prepared to seduce him. I scheduled an emergency appointment with my stylist Keith who always kept me tight. After getting my hair done, I would get a Brazilian wax before going to Victoria Secret to pick out a couple sexy things.

Three days later, Cameron used the key card to open the door and I was waiting, ready to wheel my big fish in. With nothing to lose, I pulled out all the tricks. I was surprised Cameron was almost as good as Harris as he fucked me like he had been wanting me for years. After spending a couple days in the hotel, we checked out and took a trip to California. We stayed at a beach front home in Mission Beach for the weekend.

During that time, we continued our sexual escapades while drinking, getting high, and eating seafood. Then on the last night, Cameron seemed off. I figured he was mourning his homeboy's death. I tried to cheer him up but had no luck. Giving him some space, I went to the beach that night and sat thinking about my life moving forward.

Hours later, I watched Cameron exit the beach home. At first, he seemed to be walking towards me, but passed me like I was not there. He stopped at the water and just stood staring. I eased my way to him and placed my hand on his shoulder. Then in one move, he whipped around and wrapped his hand around my neck and forced me down into the sand. I could feel the waves beating against my feet as Cameron tightened the grip around my neck. It was dark out, but I could see his eyes. They were wild and it really reminded me of Harris. When he began to talk, the same breath that had spoken life into me was now tearing me back down.

He said that I was nothing but a gold-digging whore and would always be sold to the highest bidder. He said that he never respected a woman that would fuck the homie and abandoned their child. He said that Harris, Bennie, Effie, and Tameka were all laughing at me.

Just when I thought he was going to strangle me to death, he released the grip from my neck. Stunned, I watched him walk down the beach until I could not see him anymore. I hurried inside to find my belongings shredded and destroyed. On the nightstand there was a bus ticket back to Kansas City.

I spent my last night in the hotel crying just thinking about what happened. I was both traumatized and confused with why he wined and dined me, then tried to strangle me. He had to be crazy to spend thousands of dollars on things only to destroy them. What he did to me that night made something snap inside.

When I made it back to Kansas City, I went to Cameron's in hopes to talk to him. The door was unlocked, and I found him dead in his apartment. I left not notifying anyone. With nowhere to go and $1,000 left over from the cash he gave me, I reached out to my mother.

She found her a retired veteran named Nelson and moved in with him. He was taking care of her. You remember my cousin Maria. She hooked up with Nelson's nephew Lance who was also a retired veteran. They were finally able to live carefree with the men that took care of them. As for me, I was considered a failure in their eyes, and they did not want me around anymore.

So of course, Maria didn't answer any of my calls and my mother simply told me that I had to deal with my own problems before hanging up in my face. Feeling hopeless and angry, I wanted everyone to suffer like me, so I began to think back to where all the bad luck started. It was the night I entered Bennie's house and met Harris.

I had lost a friend, family, and my whole being. I was spiraling down and going to take some people with me. I went to my homie Wade and purchased a gun. I was going to destroy the king by taking out his queen Effie.

That night when I knocked on Bennie's front door, I did not have a plan. I wasn't sure if I would make it out alive, but I did not care. I was hoping that Tameka would be there but surprisingly she was not or at least her truck was not parked out front.

When I pointed the gun to Effie, she never stopped keeping it real. That's what I loved about her, she had heart and spoke her mind no matter what. That's probably how she was able to bag Bennie. But that no longer mattered because the love of her life is now dead. I checked the news; all they are saying is a deadly shooting. I know all three bullets hit him, but I will feel better once I'm reading his obituary.

CHAPTER SIX
RAYVIN

I was sound asleep when I received a call from Effie in a frantic. She said that Bennie had been shot and she and Lil Ben were at the North Kansas City hospital.

I headed there not knowing whether he was dead or alive, I just knew that I had to get there. When I arrived, my heart pounded as I hurried down the hall to the waiting room. When Effie saw me, she stood up and hurried to meet me. The first thing I asked was if Bennie was dead or alive. She broke down and used her free hand to take mines and begin guiding me down the hall. When we entered the room, Bennie laid still alive but hooked up to what seems to be every type of life sustaining machine in the hospital.

It was not looking good, he had taken a bullet to the abdomen, shoulder, and head. The doctors placed him in a medically induced coma for his brain to heal. The bullet to his head barely missed his Corpus Callosum. I didn't really know what that meant but it sounded serious, and I thank God the bullet missed it. Seeing Bennie like that broke me but I had to be strong for Effie who was falling apart.

I called Tameka. She was in Branson with Karris on vacation. She confirmed she was on her way back, so I ended the call and questioned Effie about what happened. She cried as she revisited what happened at the house. When finished, she laid down on the guest bed in the hospital room and rocked Lil Ben.

Once they were asleep, Rayvin went into the hall and contacted Harris. She explained what happened, and he instructed her to stay with Effie and Lil Ben and keep him posted on his uncle's condition until he arrived in two days. Harris did not want Pax to know about the shooting because it would interrupt their business, so he sat tight awaiting his first shipment of drugs.

Bennie's shooting was spreading around like wildfire and some of the dealers were concerned about a drought. They assumed Harris was dead, and Cameron was missing. Harris was sure there would be several rumors by the time he arrived in the city, but in his eyes, the more rumors floating around the less people knew the truth.

He sat back and begin to strategize on who will be the new face in Kansas City since his uncle was down. Rayvin could do the job, but he needed her to remain his hitter. He continued to think about how his uncle pulled him into the game. Now it was time for him to make some executive decisions.

Harris thought about the people in his circle, the ones he knew were loyal to him no matter what. He took a notepad and began writing down the names of his new team. When he was finished, he had five names. Rayvin who was already in and would continue to be the muscle. Tameka and Daisy would help with the distribution. May would be the legal connection. Toni had experience with drugs and knew a lot of people, so he would make her his right hand.

Learning that Loretta was responsible for the shooting, Harris would instruct Rayvin to get some out-of-town killers to handle it once they found her. He knew this would make Rayvin angry because she could taste blood, but it was a smart move because it kept them off the front line.

"Baby, is everything okay? You seem to be in deep thought," question Abriella.

"Oh, yeah, I'm fine. I just have a lot to do once the product arrives. But now that I have been kicking it with you, I am not looking forward to going back to Kansas City. I'm enjoying Florida," responded Harris.

"Let me take your mind off things. I requested a full body massage for you," said Abriella, heading to the door. When the door opened, three women entered wearing housecoats and slippers. "This is our VIP massage team for our exclusive guests."

She instructed Harris to undress and lay on the massage table. Once he was laid face up, the women took off their robes displaying their naked bodies. Abriella relaxed on the couch and watched the woman give her man the ultimate sexual massage as he laid with his eyes closed. The massage felt good to Harris, but his uncle was in the back of his mind. In Kansas City, when Rayvin saw the message about out-of-town hitters, she was pissed.

Rayvin

I don't understand why Harris won't let me drop the hoe myself. He didn't let me in on Cameron, he does not want anything to happen to Twyla. He wants me to let his twin cousins from Chicago, Kenneth and Barry, handle Loretta when I can simply find her and plant a bullet in her head. This is the worst thing since Rachel's death. I feel like these hoes are out here trying us and they need to be checked sooner than later.

When I think about Twyla and Loretta, I taste blood. Things were simple when Harris was just hustling and getting money. Now Harris is falling fast for females and these bitches are becoming deadly. Abriella is Harris's new woman, and he is diving in headfirst like he didn't learn from Twyla.

I am concerned where Harris's head is because he has always been calculating with the women he chose. The dysfunction started with Loretta who ended up trying to kill Bennie. Twyla had him being rescued from a shallow grave. Now we have Abriella and she's more powerful than him because she's a part of his money flow. So, if he fucks her over and we lose, then we will have to go up against the Cartel.

Rayvin went to the hospital door and peeked inside to check on Effie and Lil Ben. They were still asleep. She looked at Bennie and tears began to run from her eyes. She had to be strong for Effie and Lil Ben but now that they were asleep, she could let her emotions flow. She stood in the door and cried for several minutes thinking about Bennie and the good times they shared. Based on the doctor's assessment, they were not hopeful that he would pull through.

CHAPTER SEVEN
TAMEKA

Harris returned to Kansas City after receiving the product from Pax for distribution. When he arrived, per his request, Tameka was waiting at the private airport to pick him up. She stood outside her SUV watching him load the vases filled with keys of cocaine in the trunk. Harris gave her a warm hug before hopping into the driver seat. When finished, Tameka settled in the passenger seat while Harris started the engine and sped away. The next stop was Bennie's house to drop off the product before heading to the hospital where everyone was.

"How is my uncle doing?" questioned Harris.

"He's holding on. The doctor said they want to keep him under for three weeks to allow time for the bullet wound in his head to heal. He is going to need a colostomy bag for a few months, and he will undergo physical therapy later for his shoulder," spoke Tameka, wiping her tears.

Harris placed his hand on her leg in attempt to comfort her while focusing on the road.

"Don't worry Bennie is a fighter. We will all get through this as a family. I really need you right now, Tameka, and you already know I got you," said Harris.

"I know you got us. I am just worried about what's going on because you were missing, now Cameron is gone, and Bennie is shot. It's like karma is coming back full force."

Harris turned off the truck radio and instructed her to turn off her phone before speaking, "Don't worry about Cameron. I killed him because he and Twyla's ass tried to kill me. That bitch is somewhere laying low. They took all the money out of one of my safes. But it's cool because I can bounce back from that. As for Loretta! Shit that bitch been crazy, but I really didn't expect her to go this far."

"Effie said that bitch was talking about everyone was turning against her. I can't believe she would do this to her friend," responded Tameka.

"I wish I never fell weak to her flesh. Then we had a beautiful daughter together. I am just thankful I was able to get custody of Karris and now she has a wonderful mother," responded Harris, patting her on the shoulder.

"Never regret how it happened. If it was not for that crazy bitch, I would not be blessed with a daughter. You know God places things in our life for a reason," said Tameka before giving him a soft punch in the arm.

A half hour later, Harris turned into an alley and drove until he reached Bennie's garage. After parking inside, he and Tameka unloaded the vases and locked them in a secret cellar under Bennie's garage. Next, they locked up and hurried to the hospital.

Tameka

The past three weeks have been stressful, and I am thankful that Harris is not dead. Karris kept asking for her father and I really didn't know what to say. Now that he is back, I feel secure and ready to face anything. This situation is proof that no matter what we go through we are family, and we will always have each other's back.

Arriving to the hospital, Harris hurried inside and took the stairs to the ICU on the 4th floor. As soon as Effie saw him hurrying down the hall, she started guiding him towards Bennie's room. When Harris entered, he gasped at the sight of his uncle laying in the hospital bed hooked up to several machines. When Daisy and their three daughters entered the room, they found him kneeling on the side of his uncle's bed.

Harris

Ever since I got the call about my uncle, I have been trying to keep a straight face and hide my emotions. When times get tuff, he used to always say, "eat the shit now then throw it up later because the world will never stop spinning on the account of you." So, I have been holding shit down and now I was with my family.

Harris grabbed Bennie's hand; it was cold and clammy. While he continued to stare down at his uncle, Harris began hallucinating. Suddenly, the bed turned into a coffin. His breathing became labored, and he began shaking his head rapidly. He stumbled back while holding his chest. Cassandra came in the room; she rushed to him and wrapped her arms around him.

"It's going to be okay, son. Bennie is a fighter," Cassandra whispered.

Harris took a seat in the chair next to the hospital bed, never letting go of his mother. He sobbed until the doctor entered requesting for everyone to meet in the conference room. When Harris walked in the room, May, Toni, Rayvin, and the children were already inside waiting.

The doctor waited patiently for everyone to get settled before speaking, "As we discussed before we are going to keep Mr. Grimes in a medically induced coma. I also have some good news. In the past few hours his numbers have improved significantly. If this continues, we will start removing him from the machines in the next few days."

After confirming that no one had any questions, the doctor exited the room.

Harris walked over to the window and gazed out at the cloudy sky. Now taking everyone away from Kansas City made more sense. He did not want to risk anything else happening to anyone in his circle again. He was going to be spending more time in Florida and the plane trips could not get him here fast enough if something else happened. He turned and looked at everyone in the room.

"We are stronger together than apart. It's time to leave Kansas City and make some real moves. Tameka, you've been talking about moving back to North Carolina. Start looking for a place and spare no expense. I have a couple of other stashes to use if you need more money. Daisy, go to Atlanta and start your business. May, go to Texas and enroll Junior in the school we were talking about. Rayvin, you already know your role, you will remain my hitter. Effie, once my uncle can travel, you are moving to Tampa, Florida. Bennie has already placed an offer on two houses he was interested in. Toni, you are hanging with me because you know the drug world," Harris finished.

"What are we going to do about Loretta?" Tameka whispered, not wanting the children to hear that part of the conversation.

If you are wondering why such intense conversations are being held in front of the children, it's because Bennie and Harris did not believe in withholding information from their children. If they were exposed to it at an early age, they could be taught how to handle it. That had always been the Grimes way and so far, it had not failed them.

"Oh, she's going to get handled. We just need to find her," responded Rayvin.

"Well, if we can't find her, let's hit her where it hurts. Maybe her mother or Cousin Maria, I know they live in Belton, Missouri," said Tameka.

"That bitch does not care about her family," responded Effie.

"What about me?" questioned Cassandra.

Harris wrapped his arms around his mother and spoke, "Mom, pick a place to live, and make sure you have enough room for all your grandkids and nephew."

Harris gestured for Toni and Rayvin to follow him. They exited the hospital and got inside Tameka's SUV and drove to Bennie's to prepare for the drop offs.

Back at the hospital, Cassandra, Daisy, May, Tameka, Effie, and the children continued to hang out in both the waiting areas not far from Bennie's hospital room. If everyone stayed quiet, the nurse agreed to not make them leave after visiting hours.

"So, Daisy, looks like I will no longer have to hear about how Harris kept you from your dream to own a business in Atlanta," said May, never taking her eyes off her laptop screen.

Daisy rolled her eyes. "Look, don't start this drama, we all need to stick together and support Effie."

"You know that's what I hate about you, Daisy. You always talking about sticking together and putting Harris on a fucking pedestal instead of seeing him for the filthy dog he has been to all of us. He left us all hanging for a bitch he barely knew, and she tried to kill him," said May.

"Did you not hear me, miss law degree! I said we need to stick together for Effie and Lil Ben. Why are you trying to find a reason to bring up an issue with Harris?" Daisy fired back.

"That's because this is really about Harris. Destiny told me you were not taking the wedding well. She also told me that Harris had to come console you after the wedding rehearsal," spoke Tameka.

May gave Destiny a scolding look before countering, "Yeah, my wounds are still fresh, but the fact still stands that Harris left all of us for Twyla. Now that she has stabbed him in the back, he is running back to us, needing us to ban together like some Power Rangers."

"May, the only thing we lost was Harris's dick, not his heart nor his money. You know he is a good father and provider if anything," said Tameka.

"Oh, my fragile Tameka, I am sure you know all so well about that. How many times has he put you on the back burner for another woman especially a ghetto hoe like Loretta," said May.

"I figured you would say that and to be honest, I never looked at it that way. Harris has always been my family no matter what was going on between us," responded Tameka.

"Don't waste your breath on this bitter bitch, she is blinded by emotion and thinks she is better than us," said Daisy.

"If that isn't the truth then I don't know what is," said Cassandra, interrupting the argument.

"Miss Cassandra, it's not like that I am just—"

May's words were cut off by Harris's mother who continued, "May, since we are stating facts, let me take the time to tell you that I never cared much for you. You walk around like you did Harris a fucking favor because you are lawyer. Harris didn't need your money for the record. I'm not saying he was a saint, but you will not stand in this hospital in front of his children and talk down on him. So, either you are in or out. Tighten up, you little uppity bitch, or get the fuck off the bus." She left the room.

"Well, let the church say Amen," joked Tameka, clapping her hands.

May rolled her eyes and continued typing on her laptop. Cassandra's words stabbed deep. But she truly felt that she was the best woman Harris ever had. She was still hurting about him leaving her for Twyla. But she had to face facts that the women she was calling stupid had already been through what she was going through with Harris.

In the hall, Cassandra refilled her cup of espresso. She was worried about her brother and praying this was not his final karma. If Bennie died, she would be the one everyone looked up to moving forward and that made her nervous because she had a history of falling apart and not being dependable.

Cassandra

I sit back and watch these ladies. It's a complete reality show at times. Let's start with May, as you can see, I am not too fond of her stuck-up ass, and you probably are not either. She thinks she is better than most because she has a college degree but that's not the type of shit I acknowledge in our world. You can be just as smart and successful without that BA, MA, or PhD behind your name. Now don't get me wrong, I love to see all women especially black women be successful. But that bullshit May dishing out in that conference room is disrespectful and the only thing that is saving her narrow ass is my grandson's existence.

Now Tameka, that's my girl. She has always been down to earth, nurturing. I remember her mother, Tammy. She and I used to drink and do drugs together. Tammy would talk about her daughter so much, I felt like I already knew her when I met her in person. If I had to describe Tameka I have two words, "beautifully imperfect."

Toni is just broken by life and has succumbed to it. But one thing is that she is honest and loyal. She never played the white girl card with my son, and I appreciate that.

Now Rayvin! She is not the one to play with and I am glad she is on our team. I've heard that she and Harris had something in the past but that is clearly not happening now because any bitch in her way would probably be dead.

Harris's childhood sweetheart Daisy. I remember watching them chase each other all around the projects as children. It was like everyone knew they were an item and with that came a lot of lies and hating. Most of the time Harris was accused of sleeping with girls that he would not touch with a ten-foot pole.

And Cookie, though she had no business fucking with my son, I still hate what happened to her. I know how it feels to fall for someone who rejects you. Trust me a broken heart will have you in a dark place. I remember Harris's father left me so empty.

I was surprised to learn that Twyla was her daughter. I knew she had a daughter, but she never allowed her out the house unless she was coming or going. I know it broke that little girl to watch her mother spiral out of control. Then she found her dead, that had to be traumatizing.

If it was not for my family, then I would have still been on drugs and probably committed suicide myself. I remember Bennie would hunt me down and try to convince me to come home. He would give me pictures of Harris and update me on how he was doing. When he talked about my son, he would light up like it was his child. My sister Rachel was like a storm. She would find every spot I was at and cause drama and confusion. Things got so bad that the drug dealers and crackheads hated to see me coming.

I took my family through so much with my addiction. But to support someone with a drug addiction, you must be able to love them at their worst. My family's love was greater than my addiction. It was days they had to just love me because there was no way to get me straight. It was days that I disappointed them beyond anything, and they still accepted me. My mother was on her death bed and used her last God given breath to plead with me to stop doing drugs. If it were not for my families' strength like I said before, I would still be on drugs or dead.

Now I may lose the only rock I have left, and I am terrified because I would no longer have anyone to lean on. I know my son will look out for me, but our relationship is still a little rocky because I won't tell him who his father is.

CHAPTER EIGHT

TONI

Toni sat in the passenger seat listening to Harris argue with May over the phone.

"May, all that mouthing off is unnecessary, we have too much going on to be worrying about the past," spoke Harris as he continued to drive. When May began cursing him out, he ended the call and allowed the phone to drop, landing on his lap.

"I don't need this type of drama," he mumbled to himself while gripping the stirring wheel with both hands.

May's attitude was the main reason why he did not want to be with her. He disliked the way she downed people especially those who he held dear to him. Reaching his last straw, he planned to have a serious talk with her in private.

"I knew May was going to be a headache from day one," said Rayvin who sat in the back seat.

Toni nodded her head in agreement while Harris continued to drive not bothering to respond. A few minutes later, he turned onto Bennie's block and parked in front of the house. Everyone exited and went inside. It was now time to prepare the drugs for distribution.

With every key of cocaine Toni touched, her craving grew stronger. Rayvin noticed the beads of sweat on her forehead and questioned, "Toni are you good? You look sick."

Toni lied and assured Rayvin she was okay. She wanted to finish preparing the drugs before talking to Harris about her struggles. Harris was so preoccupied on his cell scheduling deliveries that he did not hear the conversation nor notice that Toni was not doing so well.

Toni

I don't think I can do this. Ever since Harris went missing, I have been thinking about my life and want to change for the better. I want to be a mother to my daughter and show her the motherly love that I did not have; and for me to do that, I need to get clean.

I am not sure if Harris would agree to this. He probably assumes I have control of my addiction because I have never stolen any drugs from him. But that's only because he kept me supplied with them. Now I feel like my addiction and internal issues are getting the best of me. I don't want to fold at a time like this, but my addiction is getting stronger. When I watched my daughter crying for her dad, I wanted to be there for her. It hurt me to watch her seek consolation from May's toxic ass.

I don't want Destiny to be raised to look down on people. I want her to be smart, transparent, and strong, all the things that are not me. I know it's going to be a long road to establish a relationship with her, but I am willing to do the work, and I know that Cassandra will help me when I am ready.

Toni was relieved when they were finished preparing the drugs. After loading the truck, the three of them spent the next three hours making deliveries. Afterwards, Harris dropped Rayvin to her car and he and Toni headed back to the hospital. With the drugs finally delivered, Harris was no longer preoccupied and noticed Toni was not herself.

"You don't look well, Toni, what's on your mind?" Harris questioned.

"I want to be honest with you. I am not strong right now. I know this is the worst time, but I just need to go away and get myself together," responded Toni.

Her words took Harris by surprise because he never heard her speak of sobriety. Arriving at the hospital, he parked and turned off the engine.

"Damn that's the shit! I'm proud of you, really. I support you all the way. So, when do you want to go?"

His response made Toni cry, relieved that Harris would not be mad at her. "I have been talking to your mother and she told me all about the place she went to rehab. I want to go there because she spoke so highly of it," said Toni.

"Say no more. We can get you a flight, and I'll have mom contact the facility so we can get the ball rolling. The sooner you get clean, the sooner you can get back to your daughter because she needs you more than ever," spoke Harris.

"Thank you, Harris. I never thought you would allow me to be in my daughter's life after I messed things up so bad," spoke Toni.

"Come on, Toni, you are talking to a man whose mother struggled with addiction. Being high on drugs vs. sober displays two different people. I have always seen the high Toni. At this moment, I see the sober Toni. The real you and your heart is pure so I trust you will be a good mother to Destiny," replied Harris.

They exited the truck and went inside to the hospital cafeteria, grabbing something to eat before heading upstairs to Bennie's room. Harris took his mother to the side and explained to her what Toni wanted to do before handing her a credit card to book three flights to California. He went to May and told her they needed to talk very soon and not to leave. Thirty minutes later, Cassandra and Toni returned to Bennie's room.

"Okay, everything set up. I spoke with Marsha, and she is preparing for Toni's arrival. I found a flight that's nonstop and will take off from KCI Airport in six hours," said Cassandra, handing Harris back his card.

Harris stayed at the hospital until it was time to go to the airport. When it was time to leave, he asked May to ride with him. She nodded before heading to the restroom. Harris, Cassandra, Destiny, and Toni waited in the truck for May who took her time, realizing she was not riding with Harris alone.

When she made it to the car, Cassandra snapped on her, "If you make us miss this flight, you little spiteful bitch, I am going to beat your ass all over the airport parking lots." Cassandra promised before turning back around.

May twisted her face. She did not understand why she was a part of this trip because she never cared about Toni. At check in, she was surprised to learn that Toni would not be traveling alone, but both Cassandra and Destiny would be going. Harris gave his mother enough money for a hotel, food, clothing, and other necessary personal items.

Upset, May stood outside the terminal with her arms folded, rolling her eyes every chance she could at Toni. She felt envious that Harris was allowing Destiny to go with her mother. Cassandra noticed her scolding looks and flipped her off before going into the TSA line.

"I love you guys. Make sure you contact me the moment you land to let me know how things are going. I'll see you soon," said Harris.

He headed to the truck. When May realized he was not looking back for her, she hurried to catch up with him. Harris opened the passenger door and waited for May to get inside before closing it. He expected to argue with her about Destiny going with her mother. As soon as he was on the freeway, he fired up his blunt and drove.

Like clockwork, May began firing off at him, "I can't believe you let Destiny go with her crackhead ass mother! That bitch has never been a part of her daughter's life. Sometimes I wonder if you are slow or something."

Harris sucked his teeth. "May, that is her mother and if she is trying to get herself together, I feel like it's important for Destiny to see that."

"I don't agree with her going with a deadbeat that missed ten years of her life. Besides, she is my daughter, and her biological mother will not follow through with this rehab shit!" countered May.

"I thought you would say some bullshit because you are a hateful, arrogant, toxic, uppity bitch! Just because you have money, you think you can treat people like shit! I have been trying to spare your feelings, but the real reason why I left you was because you thought you were better than me. You talked so down on me and the people I hold dear to me. That shit is a complete turn off and you are nothing like the woman I met walking into that law office years ago. So, get off your high horse or I am cutting you out of my life and focusing only on Junior. Oh, yeah and as of now, I am informing you that Destiny is not coming back to live with you because you won't have my daughter walking around acting like your silly ass," finished Harris.

"Fuck you, Harris! You ain't shit and never will be! I upgraded you, nigga!" yelled May.

Furious, Harris yelled, never taking his eyes off the road, "Bitch, please, fuck everything about you! At the end of the day, loyalty is what matters overall. I don't like what you did at the hospital. I don't like how you talk bad about me or anyone else. We were making it before you came along, you never gave me anything I could not get my damn self!"

"You think you can just take care of your son and ignore me moving forward? You will always need me and my law degree! Remember you broke my heart and fucked my head up," said May.

Frustrated, Harris pressed the accelerator. He wanted to get May out of the truck before things got out of control.

May released a wicked laugh before continuing, "Oh, so I am toxic and the bad guy! No! I am so successful while everyone else sales dope! I should let all of you rot in prison or spit on your grave when you die."

Stunned at her statement, Harris responded, "That is it! I am done dealing with your ass moving forward. I never realized how much I hate you until now! To think I was considering marrying you before you showed me your true colors. Damn, I am glad to dodge another bullet."

His words infuriated May. She lunged out hitting him. Harris almost lost control of the truck and pulled over to the right shoulder. He put the car in park before turning to May and wrapping his hands around her neck. He choked her while speaking in a monotone voice,

"Listen to me, it's over. We have shared custody of Junior so just stay in your lane. Stay away from my family. We don't need your negative energy at the hospital. Junior is staying with me for a while and if you have a problem with that, then it's nothing to off your ass at this point."

He released the grip from her neck, placed the car in drive, and pulled back out onto the freeway. May caught her breath and for the remainder of the ride, she was silent. Instead of taking her to the hospital, Harris drove twenty minutes and parked in front of the house he once shared with her.

"What about my car? Can you at least take me up this long ass driveway?" said May in a humbler tone.

"May, get the fuck out," said Harris, never looking over at her.

"Well, fuck you too, I can do bad by myself," mumbled May before getting out the truck and slamming the door.

Harris drove away not even waiting on her to get inside. Once she could no longer see the truck in sight, she began feeling sad and lonely. She turned the key and entered her house. She dropped her purse and grabbed her cell, calling her friend. When Sybil answered and recognized May's voice, she rolled her eyes.

"To what pleasure do I owe this call?" questioned Sybil in a sarcastic voice.

"It's just been a while and me and Harris are finally done. I just need someone to talk to," responded May.

Sybil let out a chuckle. "I haven't heard from you in almost a couple years. And wasn't you and Harris done anyway because he is marrying Twyla."

"Look, I know I have been distant, but a lot has happened. I just need someone in my corner, I am all alone now," said May.

"Well, you better call your momma! You left me hanging for a nigga when I was always there for you. So, keep that same energy and never call me again because I am over it," said Sybil before ending the call.

"I deserved that," said May to herself as she went into the kitchen. She sat her cell on the counter and opened a bottle of wine.

For the remainder of the night, she sat in the dark drinking wine and listening to Mary J Blige music.

CHAPTER NINE
MAY

Tameka and Effie sat in the living room taping up the final boxes as they waited for May to drop Junior off. It was the end of January. A year and a half had gone by since Bennie was shot, and he was completing his final week of rehab so that he could travel. He decided to purchase the home in Apollo Beach, Florida and was looking forward to leaving Kansas City.

"May is taking all day to drop off Junior," said Tameka, putting tape on one of the boxes.

"Yes, she's been off her game since Harris had that talk with her. I would have loved to be a fly in the room to hear it," joked Effie.

"Yeah, but she still refused to move to Texas, so his talk didn't go too good," said Tameka.

"Like Harris said, May can stay up here by her damn self. I am sure there are some good schools in Florida," stated Effie.

"But I think it's more to it. Did you hear about her losing her job at the firm? I know she feels fucked up, that law career was her whole being," said Tameka.

"I know one of the secretaries at the firm she told me that May was off her game and cost the firm one of their big clients. They gave her a severance packet and made her resign.

Now all she does is go out and drink on the plaza every night," responded Effie.

"That's a shame. But on a good note, I spoke with Cassandra, and Toni is doing great! Cassandra is looking for a permanent spot on Mission Beach and she, Toni, and Destiny are going to live together when she gets out of rehab," replied Tameka as she looked out the window hearing May's mustang outside. She observed Junior exiting the car. He hurried up the walkway and May got out the car and followed close behind.

"Girl! May is coming to the door. I wonder what that is about she never gets out," said Tameka, heading to the door and opening it just in time for Junior to barge in not saying anything to anyone.

"Tameka, could I have a word with you?" asked May.

Surprised, Tameka nodded before looking back at Effie. She was grabbing her gun off the shelf. She went to the door with the gun by her side before speaking, "May, you are not on that Loretta shit are you?"

When May shook her head, Effie rolled her eyes and handed Tameka the gun before walking away. Tameka stepped out onto the front porch and took a seat in the chair.

"I see the house sold," said May. When Tameka didn't respond she continued. "Look, I'm not here for any problems, I just want to make peace. I know I have not been easy to deal with and I said a lot of things that hurt others, especially you. But I am so miserable. I hurt every day since Harris left me and without him my world means nothing. Now that Harris has completely cut me off, I don't have anything."

Tameka continued to listen. At first, she did not have any compassion for the woman who had stomped on her for years. But now she was seeing May in a new light and understood her pain as a woman.

"Look, May, maybe you need to take the therapy that Harris suggested. Trust me, I am an advocate that therapy works. You witnessed my struggles throughout the years," said Tameka.

May struggled to hold back tears. "I don't see the point of a therapist if it can't help me get Harris back. He said that he was going to marry me, but my attitude fucked it up."

"I remember feeling like that when Harris and I ended intimately. But at the end of the day our relationships were built on family first. As human beings, we must learn to move forward and have faith in God," said Tameka.

Her words made May smile. "You know, I wish I would have gotten to know you more at the beginning instead of being a bitch. I always thought that Daisy was the nice one, but it is you."

"Thanks for the compliment, it means a lot coming from you. But I must be honest with you, May. It's over between you and Harris and he is not reaching back for you in that way," Tameka warned.

May began to cry again. She was not able to bear the reality that Harris was done with her. "If I show him that I have changed, he will come back to me. He told me that he was going to marry me, but my attitude was the reason our relationship failed. If he still loves me, then I can get him back when I change," said May.

Tameka shook her head in pity. "May, Junior has not told you; Harris and Abriella have a baby on the way and are talking marriage."

Once again Tameka's words shattered May's hopes. Feeling defeated, she turned and walked away without saying another word.

"May, if you need to stick around for support, you're welcome to stay here. I'm not the type of person that holds your past against you, and I know what it feels like to be down. I don't feel comfortable with you leaving like this. I want you to know that there is always somebody over this way that will support you," spoke Tameka.

May turned and gave Tameka a half smile before responding, "Thanks, Tameka. You know, I always said you were weak, but you are the strongest. You know Harris was going to bring Destiny to you to take care of, but I insisted on taking her just because. I am so sorry that Majestic didn't make it, he would have had a wonderful mother. You know God will bless you for being so selfless. I am honored that my son will have you to lean on."

May walked to her car, got inside, and drove away.

Tameka went inside and Effie could see the concerned look on her face.

"What did she say?" Effie questioned.

"I'll talk about it with you in a second," said Tameka, heading upstairs to Junior.

She found Junior in the gaming room with Lil Ben and Karris watching a movie. She went into his bedroom and opened his overnight bag. She found a brown envelop that read *Tameka*. When she removed the contents from the envelope, it was a will and a life insurance policy along with both Junior and Destiny's vital records. Tameka hurried downstairs and called Harris who was in Florida.

"Hey, Harris, I think May is going to do something crazy like commit suicide," spoke Tameka, trying to speak low as possible.

Her words made Harris jump out of his seat. He questioned what happened and Tameka explained their conversation.

"I need you to go by the house to see if she is there and stay with her," said Harris.

"Okay, I am heading out now, but I really think you should get here as soon as possible. I have a bad feeling," said Tameka, regretting that she did not take May's keys. She went out the door and hopped inside her truck. She didn't bother to put her seat belt on and sped away.

Tameka kept Harris on the line while she drove to May's house. When she arrived, the car May was driving was not there. Harris instructed her to go inside, giving her the pin to the lock. But when Tameka noticed the door was ajar, she drew her gun and eased inside the house. When the automatic lights came on, the house was at a disarray.

"Harris, this is not good. The house is a mess and when Junior came home, he seemed upset. I didn't get a chance to talk to him," spoke Tameka.

"Damn, go to her parents' house. I am texting you the address now. I will call Effie and have her talk to Junior to find out what went on during his visit," said Harris before ending the call.

Tameka drove to May's parents who lived ten minutes away in hopes she would be there. When she arrived, she sighed not seeing her car. She went to the door and knocked. May's mother June opened the door and Tameka explained what happened.

June grabbed her purse and instructed Tameka to take her to the police station to file a report. The report was upgraded to an endangered person based on Tameka's encounter with May. After leaving the station, June instructed Tameka to take her to Sybil's house.

Tameka sat in the car while June talked with Sybil on the front porch. Based on her observation, the conversation looked heated. June walked away and headed to the truck. She got inside, slammed the door, and began crying. Tameka tried to comfort her the best way she could.

"Don't worry. We are going to find her," spoke Tameka. But her words did not ease June's pain.

After dropping June back home, Tameka went back home and explained to Effie what was going on. While they talked, breaking news came on the television displaying May's face.

"I hope she didn't do anything drastic," said Tameka.

"What's going on? May's face is all over the news. Where is Junior?" questioned Rayvin, closing the front door.

Tameka explained to Rayvin what was going on and they all stayed awake for the remainder of the night in hopes May would turn up somewhere.

Days passed and things were looking bad because May was not using her credit cards and there had been no cash withdraws from her bank accounts. Harris was now in Kansas City. He stayed at May's house in hopes she would return. Another week passed and the police made a visit to Harris informing him they recovered May's vehicle and there was a body inside. Harris picked up May's parents and they went to the morgue to identify the body. As Harris stood looking down at May, all he could think about was he was to blame for leaving her.

*You never know what a person is carrying so make sure your last
interaction with them won't leave you with regrets.*
Suicide is real.
If you know anyone who is struggling, don't give up on them.
Contact any support services in your city or state.
Let's help each other.

CHAPTER TEN

DAISY

Today is the day of May's funeral services. Her death has me in total shock.

She was arrogant and strong minded about everything. I guess Harris was her weakness like he had been to all of us. When she was going off at the hospital, I understood where her anger came from. I always thought that Toni would be the one to commit suicide but surprisingly she is now sober and on track. May's death takes me back to Cookie and how she killed herself because Harris broke her heart. I prayed to God many days that I would never get to that point.

Junior must go throughout life knowing that his mother gave up on him. Don't get me wrong, we all have his back. But no one will ever be able to erase what happened and replace his mother.

Four weeks ago, I remember receiving the call from Effie informing me that May was missing, and it was not looking good. I called Harris to check on him and he told me that he was heading to Kansas City. He wanted me to have my mother to look after the girls and come. I booked a flight and arrived early that following afternoon. When I arrived at the airport, he picked me up and took me to May's house.

When I went inside, I was shocked to see her house so messed up because May was obsessed with cleaning. We cleaned up the mess and the plan would be to sit until she came back. I assumed Harris wanted me to be there because in the past, May and I were once cool with each other.

While we were waiting, we talked about he and May's relationship and what went wrong. I could tell that he really loved her. When he told me that he almost married her, I felt envious and began to argue with him. I questioned why we could not make it together with knowledge that I was scratching an old wound. Harris went into the kitchen to retrieve a bottle of wine and two glasses. When he returned, he invited me to join him on the deck. The February air gave me a chill but the very firepit that May burned Harris's belongings kept us warm.

Harris poured our wine and tried to avoid my question by talking about our daughters. I gave him a quick update before focusing back to the question. He reminded me that I was his first real love, and I would always have a place in his heart. We both ended the conversation agreeing that we are better as friends. It made me feel good to hear that reminder because honestly, I wasn't sure where his head was at these days.

I spent years trying to find a man that would make me feel the way that he did. There was only one that could fill the shoes and that was Lewis. When I relocated to Atlanta, I was fortunate to reconnect with him and we are currently together. Things are moving fast but I don't mind because he keeps me happy.

Lewis has also been a big support to me, and I feel secure with him. He is well established and owns several commercial properties in Atlanta, even the building I'm currently conducting my business out of. I pay him rent even though he keeps reminding me that I don't have to. Harris taught me to never take handouts and that's what I live by. See, that's what I will always love about him, he was a great friend.

Back to that night.

Although Harris reassured me that he loved me, and we would always be family no matter what, I was still not ready to tell him about Lewis being back in my life. I knew hearing his name would make him angry. It was a must have conversation that we would need since Lewis was around our daughters. But now it was more important to find May and I did not want to add any more stress to his plate.

We stayed in May's house for days and the night before the cops came, we drove around hoping to find her. I know we both felt like she was dead, but we would not allow our minds to settle enough to accept it. We ended up going to her favorite bar downtown and getting drunk until we were too numb to think about her. Then we drove drunk back to May's house. Pulling in her driveway and not seeing the car she was driving sobered us up. That night we didn't want to be alone, so we decided to sleep in the guest room together holding one another.

Our emotions were high and early the next morning we ended up having sex. Have you ever wondered why no matter what is going on in your life there is always room for sex? Well, my analogy is that it's the next best thing to faith because it is free and feels good no matter what is going on in your life.

But afterwards for the first time ever, I regretted it. Harris must have felt the same way because when we were done, he sat at the edge of the bed and told me that he had a baby on the way with a woman named Abriella. This was the first time I ever heard of this bitch and my heart shattered. I reacted out of emotion and went ahead and told him that Lewis and I were together.

Harris was silent for several seconds as I laid there staring at his bare back awaiting his reaction. Then he turned around and the fury in his eyes startled me. He stood from the bed and punched a hole in the wall. He yelled that he was tired of going through all these changes. Fed up, I sat up and yelled back, reminding him that he was the one making all the changes and causing so much confusion. I took the opportunity to remind him that this shit started with Cookie's death. He was fucked up and that's why his relationships were always dysfunctional. I told him that even though he meant well, that his relationships would continue to fail until he changed the way he did things.

As I spoke, he stood looking at me allowing the tears to fall from his eyes. It was a hard pill to swallow but he needed a reality check. I told him he needed professional help, or his path of destruction would continue. I needed him to think about his daughters and how this karma could play out through them later.

He dropped to his knees and explained to me that he was trying to fix everyone and prevent what happened to Cookie.

After sitting in silence for several minutes, he looked up at me and gave Lewis and I his blessing. I thanked him that morning for releasing my heart.

Our conversation was disturbed by someone beating on the front door. Harris looked at the surveillance and it was two men wearing suits. I was sure they were detectives, so I dressed and hurried to the balcony looking down into the living room, being careful not to be seen. It took my breath to hear the detectives say that they found May's car and likely her body inside. They requested Harris to come to the morgue to make a positive identification.

When the detectives were gone, Harris dressed and left me at the house without saying one word. I didn't feel comfortable staying at May's house alone, especially after confirmation that she was dead. I called an uber and headed over to Bennie's. When I arrived, I didn't tell anyone that I had been in town all week and was present when Harris found out about May. It was horrible sitting for hours knowing that she was dead. Then Harris arrived and delivered the bad news.

The hardest thing for me was to witness Harris trying to tell Junior that his mother was never coming back. Junior lashed out at his father, blaming him for breaking his mother's heart. After calming him down, Tameka held Junior as he sobbed while Harris sat on the front porch in the cold crying. I contacted my mother and instructed her to fly the girls to Kansas City before joining Harris on the porch and consoling him. When he looked at me through bloodshot eyes, he told me that I was right. This was his karma and he had fucked up everyone's life being a selfish man. He now understood that to break the cycle, he had to let go and repent.

The days leading to May's services were rough for everyone. Junior was not doing well, and Harris had mentally shut down. Cassandra was not coming back until Toni was approved for release from rehab to travel. Bennie was discharged from the rehabilitation center and his presence alone just gave everyone comfort. Rayvin stopped by frequently throughout the day, while keeping the money straight out in the streets.

After the funeral service, everyone would leave Kansas City and I was okay with that because this city was full of nothing but stress and heartache. After the movers came and removed all the belonging out of Bennie's house, we all checked into the Harrah's hotel and tried to relax. Lord, today I pray that my family makes it through this so that we can get out of here for good.

May's Funeral

Everyone exited the hotel rooms and quietly headed down to the lobby where two SUVs were waiting to transport them to the church. At the church, Cassandra and Toni stood outside waiting while smoking cigarettes.

When we arrived and Harris saw Toni, he gave her a hug, impressed on how she looked. Now sober, her face was fuller, and she looked healthy. Bennie tried to fire up a cigarette, but Effie snatched it from his hand. When everyone entered the lobby, the funeral staff escorted them into the sanctuary. As they walked down the aisle, everyone stood and watched them.

Instead of taking a seat, Junior went to his mother's casket and stared down at her. He had never seen her look so peaceful in his life. He hoped that she would get up any second and start yelling at him like she had always done. He frowned at her attire knowing that his grandmother June dressed her like she was an usher. He turned to his grandparents and yelled, "Why do you have my mother dressed like this!"

Shocked, everyone in the sanctuary began to whisper to each other about the outburst while June cried uncontrollably. Junior did not care what people thought because it was his mother who was dead. He thought about the last time he spent with her. He knew something was off because she was too easygoing about everything that weekend.

She had taken him to his favorite restaurant on the Plaza where they had all you can eat seafood. Then Saturday she cooked his favorite, oxtails. The two of them spent time watching movies and playing video games. They talked about life, and she told him how proud she was of him. That weekend was the best time of his life. The thing that stood out was the house not being clean as usual. When he tried to clean up, she stopped him and ensured she would get a maid service to come that Monday.

On Sunday, Junior awakened finding it odd his mother did not wake him. When he went to her room, he found her smoking crack. They argued and he threatened to tell his father. She told him she needed the drugs to ease the pain of a broken heart. She pushed him out the bedroom and spent the day behind locked doors until Junior insisted that she take him to his Uncle Bennie's house. When Effie asked him about what happened during his visit, he told her that everything went great.

Junior's thoughts were disturbed by his father placing his hand on his shoulder. He turned, snatched away from him, and ran out the sanctuary. Harris started to go after him, but Bennie stopped him.

"Nephew, let him have a moment to blow off the steam and I will go talk with him. You go ahead and say goodbye to May. I know you are hurting and trying to be strong for everyone," spoke Bennie.

Harris went over to May. He agreed with his son, she was dressed horribly wearing a skirt and jacket suit. The attire reminded him of an usher. Her hair and makeup were perfect, and she looked so peaceful. He kissed her lips before whispering that he was sorry. He returned to his seat and stayed there for the remainder of the service.

Out front, Bennie smoked a cigarette while sitting with Junior.

"Uncle Bennie, why did my mother have to die?" questioned Junior.

"G-Nephew, don't question why she died because we will all die," responded Bennie before taking another drag of his cigarette.

"Then why did my father make my mother sad? She told me her heart was broken," said Junior.

Bennie shook his head in pity. He hated that May exposed their son to she and Harris's personal life. He knew that would always keep a wedge between Junior and his father's relationship.

"I remember when someone took my father's life when I was a teenager. I was angry and asking why all the time. But at the end of the day, I didn't find peace until I accepted that it was his time to go. When my mother died, it hurt more because she was the one that nurtured me and allowed me to be emotional. I was still very young when she left us also," said Bennie.

"How did you get through losing my great grandmother?" inquired Junior.

"I just took it one day at a time. Your father was one of the reasons why I kept pushing because I had to be there for him. You just keep pushing to find peace in this. And remember it's not your fault and we will all be there for you," said Bennie.

"My grandmother June dressed my mother like an old church lady," said Junior.

"Well, we all know your mother was not an old lady. But that's your grandmother's taste. So let her have that because she misses her daughter just as much as you miss your mother. Now what are we going to do about your father?"

"He is the reason why she was unhappy and doing drugs. Why didn't he just stay with her?" said Junior.

"Your grandfather broke your grandma Cassandra's heart, and it took an army to get her to a better place. At the end of the day, your mother had a choice to at least live for you. We are not going to put everything on your father. Your father loves you so don't spend the rest of your life punishing him for something you had no control over," said Bennie.

They both sat outside for a few more minutes before Junior stood up, then held out his hand to help Bennie up.

"Can you walk me back inside so I can say goodbye to my mother?"

"Sure, but on one condition, you have to hug your grandma June and apologize for that outburst," said Bennie, taking his hand.

Junior used his weight to assist with helping his uncle. When they turned to go inside, Rayvin was standing with the door open waiting.

"We are waiting for you, Junior, to come say goodbye to your mother," said Rayvin.

They went inside and Bennie walked Junior to the casket. Afterwards, Junior went over to June and gave her a hug before apologizing. He went over to his father and sat next to him. He grabbed his hand without saying a word. Harris leaned in and whispered the words sorry. Junior didn't respond, he just continued to look forward at his mother's casket while the funeral staff said final prayers.

Bennie took a seat next to Effie and put his arm around her. He looked around at his family. He was looking forward to leaving Kansas City and watching his family flourish in new places.

CHAPTER ELEVEN
EFFIE

It was mid-August when Rayvin found out where Loretta was living. She intentionally kept the information from the twins because vengeance would belong to Effie. But she had to pay Kenneth and Barry hush money and agreed to explain everything to Harris.

After landing at the airport, Effie used a fake ID to reserve a rental car and drove to meet up with Rayvin. They headed straight to Loretta's where they witnessed her leaving her apartment building located in the downtown area. They followed behind the white BMW as she ran errands.

"Looks like she finally found a sugar daddy," joked Effie.

Two hours later, Loretta returned to her apartment. When she entered the parking garage with her keycard, Rayvin took off her seat belt and instructed Effie to park the car and meet her in the lobby of the building. She had to confirm what floor Loretta was getting off on.

As instructed, Effie hurried and parked before walking into the lobby trying to look casual. She had to admit she was nervous. Rayvin was standing looking at the names on the mailboxes.

"You know the best thing about this covid 19 pandemic is that the mask conceals our faces," said Effie, pointing to the mailbox with Loretta's name on it.

"Okay, cool. The elevator stopped on the 4th floor so let's take the stairs," said Rayvin.

They hurried to the stairwell and climbed the stairs until they reached the 4th floor.

"Damn, I need to work out more," said Effie, pulling her mask down for a moment to catch her breath.

"You been doing the upper body workouts and going to the range weekly, right?" quizzed Rayvin.

"Yes, I have," answered Effie, following her down the hall.

When they reached apartment 417, Rayvin went to knock but Effie stopped her.

"Let me go inside alone. I need to deal with this by myself," spoke Effie, knocking on the door.

She covered the peephole so the Loretta would not see her. When the door opened, Effie pushed her way inside, closing the door behind her. Loretta opened her mouth to scream but was silenced by Effie who smacked her with the gun.

"You really have nerve still living in Kansas City after you shot my husband," said Effie.

In the hallway, Rayvin could not help herself, so she eased inside the apartment. She figured since she would not be the one pulling the trigger, at least she could witness Loretta die.

Once inside, she smiled wickedly at the sight of Loretta pleading for her life, "Look, Effie, I am so sorry. I was angry and acted out of emotion." She cried.

"Oh, so now you want empathy. You didn't seem to care about my tears when you tried to kill my husband in front of his wife and child," responded Effie, screwing on the silencer.

She pointed the gun and pulled the trigger twice. Both bullets went into Loretta's heart. Effie stood over her and watched her until she took her last breath.

Rayvin crept from the shadows. "Good job! You were straight to the point just like what I would have done," she finished, turning the air conditioner down to 60 degrees.

They combed the apartment making sure there were no cameras before exiting and taking the elevator down to the lobby.

They walked casually out the building holding hands like they were a couple. When outside, they walked at a fast pace down a half a block to where the car was parked.

"Are you good? This is your first time, and it can be rough," questioned Rayvin, starting the car and driving away.

Effie gave her a nod and looked out the window. Everything happened fast and she did not know how to feel now. While processing, she focused on remaining calm.

On the way to the airport, they made a stop at the bottoms to toss the guns into the Missouri River. At the airport while Effie turned in the rental, Rayvin changed her clothing in one of the restrooms. Effie joined her in the bathroom and changed her clothing. They checked in at the counter for their flights and went through TSA.

On the flight, Rayvin relaxed with her eyes closed. Effie sat quietly staring out the window into the darkness. Killing Loretta ran through her mind like a movie. After delivering the shots, Loretta stared at her estranged friend until she took her last breath. During that time, Effie was too numb to acknowledge the sorrow in her eyes, but now that her adrenaline was down, reality was setting in and the image was more vivid. Then memories of the good times she shared with her began to flood her thoughts bringing her to tears.

"It's hitting you hard now, isn't it," questioned Rayvin, now opening her eyes.

"Yes, but I would have still did it all the same," responded Effie, wiping her tears.

"Trust me, I get it. That's why I keep asking you if you are okay," said Rayvin.

She flagged down the flight attendant and ordered two double shots of scotch. When the flight attendant returned with the drinks, she handed one to Effie.

"Drink this down. It will help you relax a little," instructed Rayvin before taking her shot to the face and repositioning herself in the first-class seat.

Effie took the drink and tried to sit back and close her eyes to relax. Once again, visions of Loretta flooded her mind.

"Just let the visions play out. It's going to be a long time before you can close your eyes and not see her," whispered Rayvin.

"I know, I read about it in a psychology book," responded Effie.

Rayvin opened her eyes and gave her a questioning look before chuckling, finding it funny that Effie was reading on the side effects of killing someone. "Shit, you need to show me that book," joked Rayvin, playfully nudging her.

Effie took in a deep breath and tried to close her eyes again. She took Rayvin's advice and allowed the visions of Loretta to run torment in her thoughts. To the day she first met Loretta to the night of the shooting. She ordered another double shot of liquor.

The Next Day

In Kansas City, Cameron's father sat in a local bar enjoying a beer and some hot wings when breaking news appeared across the screen.

"Local police are investigating a homicide in a downtown Kansas City apartment building. The body is identified as Loretta Scott. Police are working the scene and have no leads. If you have any information, please call the tips hotline at 816-865-0000."

Kevin was shocked remembering Loretta. It reminded him of Cameron. It was the worst pain having to bury a child. A lot of time passed since his son's untimely death. Kevin remembered the morning a neighbor contacted him and told him that a dead body was found in the apartment after complaints of blood dripping from the ceiling into the apartment below. When Kevin made it to the scene, it was taped off. He waited in the crowd for hours until they brought out the body.

He recalled Loretta approaching him. She wore a hat pulled down concealing her face. She told him that it was Bennie because Cameron and Twyla had killed Harris. She also told him that she was the one that shot Bennie. Hearing that Harris was dead made Kevin feel ill and he wondered why he had not heard anything. They parted ways and he spoke with the detective who said that the body looked like Cameron's, but he wanted Kevin to come down and make a positive id.

Later that night, he sat on the computer looking up funeral home websites to find Harris's obituary but had no luck.

The thought of both of his sons being dead had him in tears. He wondered how things would have been if he would have simply stepped up and claimed Harris. He could have raised them together, but he would not have Melba.

Kevin snapped out of his deep thoughts realizing he was still at the bar. He paid for his food and exited the establishment. Loretta's death had him on edge so he would go warn Twyla so she could keep his grandson safe.

CHAPTER TWELVE

NO

Harris and Junior sat in the attorney office waiting for May's parents to arrive. Months had passed since May's death and Harris was not sure why he had to attend the reading of a will assuming everything was resolved. May's parents entered; they only greeted their grandson before taking a seat.

"Okay, Mr. Douglas, go ahead. Let us get this over with," instructed June, giving Harris a nasty look.

She was upset because May had willed everything to Harris and created a clause in the custody agreement that in the event she died, her parents could not gain custody of her son.

Mr. Douglas cleared his throat and began to read, "This is the last will and testament of May Grace Adams.

I, May Grace Adams, grant sole custody to Harris Grimes the birth father of my son Harris Grimes Jr.

This arrangement cannot be reversed by anyone especially my parents Rufus Adams and June Adams. If Harris Grimes is unable to care for Harris Grimes Jr., I grant sole custody to Tameka Davis."

Mr. Douglas paused and looked around the table to make sure there were not questions before continuing,

"I, May Grace Adams, will my two vehicles and portion of house to Harris Grimes. My Cash investments and bank accounts will be divided in half and given to Harris Grimes and Harris Grimes Jr.

In addition, when I die, by no means allow my mother to dress me." Mr. Douglas struggled to keep in his laugh as he looked up at June who rolled her eyes.

"Well, that's too late, daddy," whispered Junior. Harris gave him a playful nudge and advised him to save the wise jokes for after the meeting.

Infuriated, June and Rufus stood from the table and exited without saying goodbye. When they were gone, Mr. Douglas handed Junior twenty dollars and told him to go to the cafeteria to get some snacks while he discussed some things with his father. When Junior reached the door, Mr. Douglas's secretary was waiting to escort him to the cafeteria.

"Harris, I know you are wondering why we are here months later discussing this will. Well, June has been using all her connections to prevent the reading of it. I did not trouble you with it because you have enough on your plate dealing with Junior. I knew it would be resolved once the right judge received it," spoke Mr. Douglas.

"Why am I not surprised," said Harris. He got up before confirming the meeting was over. He went to the cafeteria and joined Junior who was still selecting his items.

Harris

One thing I can say is that May is fair when it comes to business. She loved that house, so I plan to remodel it and use it as a family home when we are in Kansas City. Right now, my priority is taking Junior to meet Abriella who is carrying my son. I plan to propose and marry her soon. Despite losing May tragically, and Bennie's shooting, our family's come back has been outstanding. Business is good with Pax, and we are getting more money. I told Uncle Bennie to just retire and let me handle things moving forward because he deserves a break.

I am thankful that I have an uncle like him. He stepped up at a young age to be my father and just figured it out. He used his heart to guide him and taught me how to survive and get money. Yeah, he made some mistakes like exposing me to all the wrong shit at an early age. Everyone knew that if they fucked with me, they had to see Bennie. He was dedicated to me no matter what I did. He stayed getting me out of trouble when I made stupid decisions. People envied the love he gave me, and I never wanted for anything. I was so good that I wasn't even tripping off my father. Just messing around as a teenager, I asked my mother about my father and her very words were "he doesn't matter" and she walked away. When I brought it to Uncle Bennie, he never really wanted to discuss it either.

Harris and Junior headed to the airport to fly back to Florida. Junior thought he was going back to stay with Bennie and Effie. But Harris was ready to take him home to meet

Abriella. He enrolled him in a private school and looked forward to spending his days being a soccer dad in between business.

Now days the little things mattered to him. After almost dying, he wanted to surround himself with love and happiness.

Junior sat on the bench playing his Nintendo DS while his father checked their bags in. When finished, Harris grabbed a Red Bull and Junior an orange juice before returning to the bench where his son0020 was still focusing on his video game. They went to the terminal and sat until it was time to board the plane.

"Hey, Junior, I want you to come live with Abriella and me. She will be giving birth to your little brother soon, and we can be a happy family," spoke Harris.

Junior sighed and put his earphones on, but his father snatched them off.

"Look, I know it's been a hard journey since your mother died. I just want you to know that I love you and we are going to be okay," spoke Harris.

"I really miss her. Why did God do this to me," said Junior.

Hearing those words made a knot form in Harris's throat. He struggled to hold back tears as he tried to figure out how to respond to the soon to be twelve-year-old. With nothing to say, he just wrapped his arm around his son and pulled him closer. The silence between them both was loud as they continued to sit waiting to board the plane. An hour later the announcement was made for first class to board.

"Come on, son, let's go home," said Harris, standing up and stretching.

He waited for Junior to get up before walking over to the short line. When they were next in line, Harris handed the clerk the tickets before proceeding onto the plane. Finding their seats, Junior sat by the window while Harris placed his bag in the overhead.

Harris took his seat, then looked over at Junior who was looking out the window at the luggage cart loading suitcases to another plane.

"Son, let's make a deal. Just give living with Abriella and I a try for a while and if you still don't like it, then you can go back and live with Uncle Bennie," said Harris, holding his hand out for a shake.

Junior looked over and smiled. He held out his hand to shake his father's before placing his headphones on and playing his video game. Once everyone was aboard and the plane took off, Harris ordered a double shot of Hennessy. He gulped it down before closing his eyes and falling asleep.

At home, Effie awakened in a cold sweat and panting. She looked up at the ceiling and took a deep breath. She closed her eyes to try to fall back to sleep. When she still saw Loretta's face, she sat up at the edge of the bed. Like Rayvin warned her, she was having nightmares of killing Loretta and sometimes the dreams consisted of Loretta as a zombie trying to kill her. Effie was so discombobulated that she did not notice Bennie still lying in bed beside her.

"What's going on with you, Effie? Ever since you returned from that girl's trip with Rayvin, you have been off," questioned Bennie, now rubbing her back.

"Everything is fine, I am just under a little stress," responded Effie.

"Come on, baby, who comes back from a girl's trip still stressed. So, you are going to just keep holding out on me?" asked Bennie.

"Baby, what are you talking about? We fucked last night," responded Effie, feeling agitated.

"Bullshit, you know I am not talking about sex! I want to know the real reason why you are not sleeping, eating much. You are drinking up the bar and smoking all my weed," countered Bennie, now sitting up on the bed before continuing,

"Do you think that I am stupid since I got shot. Something happened while you were away on that so called girl's trip. Rayvin has been avoiding my questions about it. Did you witness her kill someone?"

Effie laid back on the bed and began to cry while Bennie fired up his blunt. He sat and smoked, patiently waiting for her to finish crying so she could explain what happened. When she stopped, he passed her the weed, and she took a couple of puffs before passing it back.

"Rayvin was venting to me months ago about Harris not allowing her to kill Loretta. She said she was going to do it anyway. I told her I had to be the one that killed her because she came to my home and tried to kill you. Rayvin agreed and when she found her apartment, I flew to Kansas City to handle it. As soon as I touched down, we got right to it and left soon after. We stayed in a hotel in Miami for a couple days. Baby, I had to do it. She almost took my sanity. What If Lil Ben would have awakened, she could have shot him too. Every time I think about it, I get angry. Her envy almost shattered my happiness," said Effie.

"And that's what you think about every time you have a thought or dream about that bitch. Reminding yourself of the reason you did it will set you straight every time you feel sorry for her. You both came from rough pasts so there is no excuse she could have for causing trauma to you and your family," said Bennie, raking his fingers through Effie's long natural hair. "Promise me that if you ever have to do something like that again, you'll let me know."

"Okay, I will, but please understand that I didn't want you to stop me," responded Effie.

"Say, what! Baby, it's not what you do, it's how you do it with me. If you would have told me that's what you wanted and the reason, I would have respected your gangster and helped you to prepare."

"Well, I read a few psychology books to understand where my mental state would be after killing her," replied Effie, looking over her head at Bennie.

He laughed while pulling her to him. "I am going to need you to show me that psychology book," he spoke in a seductive voice.

They began to kiss passionately as he pulled down her gown releasing her breasts. He began sucking gently giving both equal attention. Effie moaned in pleasure while positioning herself on top of him. She grinded slowly in a circular motion on his dick until it was fully erect. She then eased on him and began riding him while moaning.

"Yes, baby, ride this dick," whispered Bennie as he stroked from the bottom meeting her thrust.

He was deep inside causing her to moan louder every time he hit the bottom. They reached their climax at the same time. She collapsed on top of him breathing hard. Suddenly, there was a knock on the door; it was Lil Ben. Effie and Bennie covered themselves just in time for Lil Ben to open the door entering the bedroom.

"Daddy, are we going to the pet store today? I need to get some fish food and you said we could get a dog," said Lil Ben, getting on the bed.

"Yes, we are, but don't you want to have breakfast first or maybe brunch?" questioned Bennie.

When Lil Ben nodded, Effie slid out of bed, pulling her gown up.

"How about chicken and waffles," said Effie, leaning over and kissing her son.

"Yay! Chicken and waffle's my favorite. Daddy, can I smoke some weed like you do every morning?" said Lil Ben.

"Yeah, you tried it," said Bennie, getting out of bed.

Effie laughed from the bathroom as she brushed her teeth. Lil Ben and his father went to his bedroom. They made it a daily ritual to talk about their daily goals while getting dressed. When finished, they went downstairs in time for Effie to finish cooking breakfast. While Bennie and Lil Ben enjoyed breakfast on the deck, Effie showered and dressed. When she was ready, she returned to the kitchen to find it was already cleaned up. She locked up and joined Bennie and Lil Ben who were waiting in the car out front.

Harris and Junior

Later that evening, when Harris parked in the driveway, Abriella hurried out to greet them.

"You must be Junior. I am so happy to finally meet you," spoke Abriella.

"Yeah, nice to meet you too," said Junior, focusing on her pregnant belly protruding through the sundress. Abriella smiled and grabbed Junior's hand then guided him into the house. When they entered, the place was immaculate reminding him of being at home with his mother.

"I didn't know what you like to eat so I just made a spread with a little bit of everything," said Abriella, stopping at the kitchen table. Junior eyes widen at all the food. "I have some ox tail soup on the stove for dinner later. Your father said you loved them." She headed upstairs to finish preparing his bedroom.

Junior grabbed a plate and began walking around the table placing assorted items on his plate. Harris washed his hands and joined his son at the table.

"How are you liking it so far?" questioned Harris.

Junior took a bite of a strawberry and gave him a thumbs up. At this very moment, Harris knew the time was right. He hurried upstairs looking for Abriella.

He wanted to plan a special proposal but, in his heart, now was the right time. He went the master bedroom and retrieved the 5-Carat ring before going to her. When he entered the room, Abriella smiled while fluffing the pillows on the bed.

"You came to help prepare the room? I need help hooking up the videogame system," she spoke, not noticing the black box in his hand containing the ring.

Harris wrapped his arms around her and kissed her neck before turning her around to face him. He kneeled on one knee and opened the box displaying the ring.

Abriella was surprised. She held her hands against her chest, staring down at Harris who spoke, "Abriella, will you marry me?"

In the moment, Abriella opened her mouth to say yes but stopped. It was the perfect proposal, but the reality was she did not feel Harris was ready for marriage. They had only been together for a short time and discussed marriage. Just not to the extent that she would accept a proposal.

"Harris, I love and want to marry you one day but not right now."

Harris closed the box and stood to his feet before going over to the window. As he stared at the ocean, Abriella continued,

"I am not saying I won't marry you. Just not right now. Ever since I met you it has been one situation after another. You always must run back to your hometown. When I ask you say everything is okay. But I can tell something is wrong because your mood changes. For us to be together, I need to know what is going on in your life. Who is your family, why can't I travel back to Kansas City with you when you go. Why haven't I met any of your children except for Junior for the first time today. I am carrying a baby for a man I don't really know."

Upset, Harris exited the bedroom without saying a word. He hurried down the hallway and ran into Junior who was looking for him.

"Come on, son, we have to leave," said Harris, guiding Junior down the stairs and out the front door to the car.

"Dad, where are we going, I wanted to see my bedroom," said Junior, getting inside the car and putting on a seat belt.

"We are going to Uncle Bennie's house. There has been a change in plans," spoke Harris, starting the car and backing out of the driveway. For the next 45 minutes they road in silence to Bennie's house.

As soon as Harris parked behind Bennie's corvette, Junior exited the car and ran through the garage into the house, making sure he announced himself before entering. Harris continued to sit inside the car replaying his proposal to Abriella. After several minutes passed, Bennie came outside to check on him.

"Hey, nephew, you good?" queried Bennie, now standing at the driver side window.

"I just need some peace and quiet," responded Harris, cradling his head.

"Well, you're not going to get it crammed up inside this Toyota. Let's go out back to the beach. It's almost my favorite time of the day, sunset," said Bennie, holding up a freshly rolled blunt.

Harris got out the car and followed Bennie out back to the private beach and took a seat on the beach chairs.

"When my mind is racing, I come back here anytime between sunset and sunrise. The water helps me clear my mind and gives me peace. Trust me, if I would have known of such solace a long time ago, I would have been moved here. I hate to say, but if it weren't for Twyla and Cameron trying to kill you, we would have never been here," spoke Bennie.

"I proposed to Abriella, and she said no. She said I have too much baggage and she need to get to know me more," said Harris.

"She is right, you have too much baggage. Moving on to a new woman won't make things better. You have a son that's grieving his mother's death and blames you for it. Destiny's mother is in rehab. Daisy has a new man around your daughters. You and your mother's relationship is still shaky. You won't face the fact that you really want to be with Tameka and let's not forget that your homie and ex-fiancé tried to kill you."

"I never had a woman tell me "No" before, so I barged out," responded Harris.

Bennie shook his head and passed Harris the blunt. "The foundation of marriage is trust, communication, love, sacrifice, respect, creativity, wonderful sex, and the truth!"

"Is that how you and Effie make it. I never seen you commit to a woman, then Effie comes, and you too take off at a fast pace. I remember when you use to run bitches in and out like crazy," said Harris before laughing.

"This is absolutely true but when Effie came along all that changed. I never believed in love at first sight, but she proved me wrong. Everything is so effortless with her, and I was not even looking for love when she came," responded Bennie.

"I wish I could figure this woman shit out," spoke Harris, taking a hit of the weed.

"Nephew, you need to get things right within yourself. I have been sitting back thinking these past few months, now considering I have more time to do it. When I think about you and all your situations, you need to know where it all started," spoke Bennie, texting Effie to bring out two glasses and the fifth of Hennessy. While he waited for Effie, he rolled another blunt anticipating the hard conversation that would follow.

Bennie had shown his nephew how to fight, kill, and hustle to survive in the streets. But now peace and clarity of self was essential, and it was time to teach this to his nephew.

Moments later, Effie came outside with the Hennessy and two cups, placing them on the table before going back inside.

Bennie poured the drinks, handing one to Harris. "Come on, nephew, it's time to have one of my real conversations." He stood and began walking closer to the water and Harris followed.

"We never talked about your father because your mother's addiction stemmed from him breaking her heart. We did what we had to do as a family to get her well and protect you. Cassandra was like Cookie and May and the only difference was the support system. We fought with your mother constantly to keep her off the ledge. The reality is that Cassandra was a side chick and when you were born, your father did not want to claim you in fear of losing his perfect relationship with his high school sweetheart who was also carrying his son. Your grandfather wanted to kill him, but your grandmother wanted to solve things with reason."

Bennie took a drink before continuing,

"But his family believed the lie he told about you not being his son. Your mother was still in love with him and so she refused to do a DNA test to prove it. Of course, that made her look suspect, so everyone believed she was just a ghetto bitch trying to trap a nigga who was going somewhere. From that point, every chance your grandfather got he made it uncomfortable for your father and his family to live in the projects. This eventually caused them to move away. I was a teenager, but I knew what was going on and I didn't like it.

Watching my sister lose her sanity and taking care of you made me stronger. I was not going to allow your father to get away free either. He was an excellent basketball player and was destined for greatness. He was the hood hero and would have made it to the NBA had I not interfered. I got him addicted to crack instead of killing him like my father wanted to. I took the pleasure in witnessing his life spiral downhill."

Bennie turned to Harris and looked in his eyes.

"Remember how Cameron would always say to you that I did not like him. Well, he was right. I could not stand him because he was one of the reasons why your father disowned you. Cameron's father Kevin is also your father. You two are brothers," Bennie finished.

Harris felt lightheaded. He dropped his glass before taking a seat in the sand. Bennie stood and watched him sit for several minutes in a daze staring at the waves. It was dark, but he could still see the water raging. He wanted to go into the waves and let the ocean swallow him. It would be better than the pain he was enduring. May and Cookie's death, his son resenting him, and Abriella refusing his proposal. The reality that he killed his own brother made him feel sick. He wondered if Cameron would have known they were brothers would he conspired with Twyla to try and kill him.

"Nephew, I am sorry, but I would have not changed what I did. The only thing I regret is not telling you who your father was sooner. I didn't want his rejection to break your spirit. But no matter how hard I tried to shield you, it still became the cause of most of the battles you are fighting today. Cameron was a casualty in the situation and Cassandra was a casualty for our family," said Bennie.

"Fuck that, you should have told me this when I told you that Cameron and Twyla tried to kill me. Where is your loyalty! How can I trust a man that has been keeping this from me all my life!" yelled Harris.

Bennie stepped closer and kneeled in front of him. He was so close the Hennessy was searing Harris's nose. Bennie spoke through gritted teeth, "Now I know this is a lot for you, but I did what is necessary for our family. If that nigga really wanted the son that I took care of all these years, then he would have stepped up even when you established a relationship with his golden child Cameron. You were never hard to find, so what stopped that coward from claiming you. I promise no pussy in the universe would keep me from claiming my seeds ever. I have been carrying this shit for years and holding you down.

So never in your life question my fucking loyalty because at the end of the day, among all the sins, I destroyed another person's life just because he didn't want you. So don't expect me to handle you tender about this, I just wanted you to know where it started so that you can get on the path of healing. Process this shit and go the fuck to therapy. At the end of the day, the blood that flows through your veins the hardest is Grimes blood. You are my son, and my grandson Junior is staying with me until you get your shit together."

He turned and picked up the glasses out the sand and began walking toward the house.

Harris watched his uncle go into the house. For the next few hours, he sat on the beach drinking the Hennessy out of the bottle. He watched the waves until he passed out in the sand. Bennie and Effie were keeping an eye on him from afar. Eventually, they came, took him inside to the guest room, undressed him, and tucked him in. Effie contacted Abriella who had been blowing his phone up and informed her that Harris was with them and okay.

Bennie

I had to make a lot of tough decisions that affected a lot of people's lives. But in my world, it's about survival; that's what my father taught me to do. Think about it, why would God put you in the same place with all these elements that are against you if he did not want you to learn to fight. I know a lot of good ole church folks would say fight with trusting the lord and keeping the faith, but what do you do when someone is holding a gun to your head. How about watching your sister sabotage herself because a nigga won't claim her baby because he worried about some pussy and his image.

It hurt me to see my nephew's reaction when he learned about his father. But I wasn't going to tolerate him snapping out on me because if I have not been nothing, I've been loyal to him all his life. Like I said before Harris is my son, and he motivated me to grind harder.

Kevin is weak, and I will never change my perception of him. Now I was starting to soften up for Cameron but after he tried to kill my nephew, I took that shit back. Harris is questioning whether Cameron would have tried to kill him if he had knowledge they were brothers. But technically homies from the sandbox are brothers and that did not stop him from violating that. That snake shit be running through people's blood, and it would not have made any difference whether he knew or not.

I can go on and on about this, but the fact is I raised Harris like my son in front of his father while he was too coward to speak the fuck up. Now I did my part letting Harris know who his father is. Now that he knows the truth, he can get on the path of healing, and I will be by his side through it all whether he likes it or not.

CHAPTER THIRTEEN
DAISY

Daisy sat upright in the hospital bed staring out the window at the unusual snowfall in Atlanta. It was the holiday season, and she was depressed because she had to spend her last month of pregnancy in the hospital; the baby was not due until the end of December. Her pregnancy had been rough, and she could not help but to wonder if the reason was because she was hiding the fact that Harris was the father of her unborn child.

Months ago, after sleeping with Harris at May's house, Daisy found out she was pregnant shortly after returning to Atlanta. On the same day she found out she was pregnant, Lewis surprised her with the proposal. When they made love that night, she made sure they used no protection. She then waited a couple weeks before telling Lewis that she was pregnant with his child.

The guilt was eating her alive and taking a toll on her health and causing a high-risk pregnancy. With plans for a spring wedding, Daisy was happy but also sad because this was the longest she ever went without seeing or speaking to Harris.

She knew he was angry with her because their daughters told him about the pregnancy and marriage proposal. Then she learned about Abriella saying no to his marriage proposal and Bennie telling him about his father. She tried to contact him, but he was not answering her calls nor responding to her text.

Their daughters went to visit often and when Daisy asked them about Harris, they told her he spent most of his time in his new beach home watching television, reading, working out, doing virtual therapy, cooking new recipes for them to try, and spending time with his children. They told their mother that they loved the new version of their father because he was spending more time with them. Daisy was happy to hear he was a on the path of healing.

"Hey, baby, why the long face? We only have three weeks to go," spoke Lewis, entering the hospital room. He held fresh flowers in one hand and a bag of food in the other. "The doctor said you can splurge once a week, so I made a trip to that restaurant Old Lady Gang since you were always talking about it." He kissed her on the forehead.

"I was wondering where you were when I woke up," said Daisy, grabbing the flowers and taking a sniff of them.

"I had some appointments and had to dash fast so I could be able to get your food. You were sleeping so peacefully that I didn't want to wake you. Have you spoke with the girls today?" questioned Lewis, getting comfortable on his fold out bed.

"Not yet, you know when they are with their father it's hard to get a call or text," said Daisy.

"Well, at least you're stuck with me until death do us part. I can't wait to see you walking down that aisle," responded Lewis, turning on his PS5.

He handed Daisy one of the controllers and they begin to play Fortnite. While they played, Daisy could not help but to continue her guilty thoughts about the baby. From the day she told Lewis she was pregnant he had not left her side. When she was hospitalized, he moved into the hospital room as well. The nurses and staff thought it was beautiful to see him so dedicated. They told Daisy that she was lucky to have a man that loved her so much.

"Damn, baby, you must be still tired because you never lose that quick," joked Lewis.

"I have been feeling odd today," said Daisy. She used her free hand to peek inside the bag of food.

Suddenly, she felt a sharp pain in her stomach causing her to drop the game controller. She laid back before rolling to her left side and began rocking trying to endure the pain. Lewis hurried out the room and returned with the nurse. A few seconds later, more staff entered the room and surrounded Daisy. The doctor came in the room and washed her hands before checking Daisy's cervix.

"Okay, we're going to let baby come if he wants to today. You have dilated to five so it will take some time but I'm pretty sure he's ready to meet his parents," said the doctor.

The doctor instructed the nurse to begin administering Pitocin to help speed up the contractions before leaving the room.

"I will call the girls and let them know the baby is coming soon," said Lewis, digging in his pocket for his cell.

Daisy winced in pain. "Baby, no, we can surprise them when they come home."

For the next seven hours, Daisy endured hard labor with Lewis by her side. At 10:07 PM on December 8, 2020, Daisy gave birth to her baby boy weighing 8 pounds 2 ounces. As she laid in her bed recovering and completing paperwork, she observed Lewis laying on his fold out bed doing skin to skin with the baby. It was both a beautiful and painful sight to see causing her guilt to lay on her heavy. She knew that if she tried to keep it a secret and it came out later, it would be worse than just telling the truth at that moment. The nurse entered the room and retrieved the paperwork before checking her vitals and leaving.

"Lewis, come over here, we need to talk, "said Daisy, patting the bed.

Lewis eased up, walked over, and took a seat, being careful to support the baby's head. He kissed him on the forehead before giving Daisy his full attention as she continued to speak,

"When I went back to Kansas City for May, Harris and I were staying in her house waiting for her to return. One night we got drunk and ended up sleeping together. Afterwards, I regretted it, and I told him about us. When I return home, I took a pregnancy test, and it was positive. Then while I was trying to figure out how to tell you, you surprised me with breakfast and proposed to me. I did not want to ruin the moment, so I did not tell you about it. I am sorry and don't want to lose you."

Daisy closed her eyes, took a deep breath, and braced herself for his reaction. While her eyes were closed, it seemed like every moment she spent with Harris taunted her thoughts. When she opened her eyes, Lewis was at the bassinet and laying the baby inside. He went to the window and began to stare at the snow. Hearing that she fell for Harris again was like reopening an old wound that healed years ago. He loved Daisy and hoped that the move to Atlanta meant she was finally over Harris.

From the moment Harris contacted her to come to Kansas City, it didn't sit well with Lewis, but he did not object. Then when Daisy told him she was pregnant, he knew she had been with someone else and prayed that it was anyone but Harris.

"Daisy, I know the baby is not mines. Years ago, when I relocated to Atlanta, I met a woman. We got serious and we were trying to have a baby. After a couple failed attempts, we consulted a fertility specialist and I found out that the hernia surgery I had as a child affected my sperm count causing it to be so low that there's no possible way I could get a woman pregnant. When you told me the news, I went with it not wanting to spoil the moment either and hoping that a miracle happened." He went back over to the bassinet looking down at the sleeping baby while continuing,

"Remember when I had that two-week business trip after I proposed to you. It was me getting away to clear my mind and process the news. I talked to my father about it. I was angry, hurt, but also overjoyed that you chose me to be this baby's father. But I am concerned about it being Harris's son."

"I love you, Lewis, and I am ready to move on with my life from Harris. I know this situation is like what happened years ago when Jamie was conceived, but I need you to believe me when I say I am moving on," said Daisy, wiping her tears away.

The baby woke up and began to cry so Lewis picked him up and begin cradling him, rocking from side to side while speaking in a soft tone,

"If you say this is my son then he is my son. But how are you going to deal with Harris on this. Among all his issues, he still is a good father, and he may not like the fact that you are hiding a child from him or the fact that another man will be fathering his child."

"Why would I tell Harris about a baby that does not belong to him," responded Daisy.

Lewis gave her a questioning look. "That's a big move, Daisy, and you need to make sure it's the one you want to make. I'm going to take care of him regardless. But I need to make sure you are really going to be able to do this."

"I'm ready to move on, I don't want to tell him anything," said Daisy, not sure if she meant it. Currently, she was only sure because Harris was not talking to her.

"Yeah, you said that years ago, but we will see," said Lewis, walking over and handing the baby to Daisy so she could feed him.

Daisy opened her mouth to respond but was interrupted by the nurse coming in with paperwork.

"Sorry to interrupt but, Miss Jones, you forgot to sign in a couple places," said the nurse, placing the papers on the cart. "And, dad, you can also sign in all the areas next to moms' signature so we can send off for the birth certificate." She left the room.

While Daisy fed the baby, Lewis shuffled through the paperwork, stopping when he saw the baby's name as Lewis Anderson. He looked at Daisy who was focusing on the baby. He smiled, it was a beautiful sight to see, and he never wanted to forget that image.

Daisy looked up and smiled before saying, "Does that answer your question?"

Lewis walked over and kissed her on the forehead. "It does but I don't want his first name to be Lewis. Let's give him your father's first name Malachi Lewis Anderson.

"I love it but are you sure you don't want a Junior?" questioned Daisy.

"Nope, I hate Juniors. It's like you don't have your own identity. Besides if the truth comes out later, I don't want Lewis to be his first name. It's cheaper to change the last name and the middle name is not always acknowledged," responded Lewis. He wasn't sure if it was a good idea for Daisy to keep the baby a secret from Harris, but he would ride with her no matter what.

CHAPTER FOURTEEN
ABRIELLA

Harris walked around the bedroom collecting assorted items and tossing it into the duffle bag. He had been living in his own place for some time and things were now looking permanent. He had no plans on returning to Abriella. Every time he took his son Adonis home, he would collect more items. At the beginning, he was taking his time in hopes of Abriella eventually coming around. But now he was tired of waiting and made the decision to move on.

The time to himself and being a full-time father was rewarding and more peaceful. It opened his mind. It made him face the man in the mirror and he gained a newfound sense of independence he had never felt before. Now he was truly living for the people that depended on him, his children.

"So, this is it, the last of your belongings. Where do we go from here?" questioned Abriella, standing in the doorway.

"Shit, you tell me because I have no idea," responded Harris, expressing agitation in his voice.

"We need more time. The therapy seems to be working. I just feel you need to —"

"Abriella, save it! I have been intentionally packing slowly for the past few weeks waiting for you to come around. I have been doing therapy while still handling my business and still it's just not enough for you. I have nothing more to give. If you are not satisfied with the man I have become, then we just need to go ahead and co-parent in peace," he finished before zipping the duffle bag.

"You know! You are right! It's time to move on. So, when it's time to pick up Adonis, I will have him at Bennie's for you," spat Abriella before leaving the room.

"Shit, that's even better," mumbled Harris, shaking his head.

He grabbed his duffle bag and exited the bedroom. He stopped by Adonis's room and gave him a gentle kiss, being careful not to wake him before leaving the house. He tossed his bag inside the trunk before getting in the car where Daisha, Clarise, and Jamie waited. He placed the car in drive and drove out of the driveway and down the street.

Inside, Abriella sat on her couch stewing with anger.

Abriella

I wanted Harris to get his shit together so we could be perfect. When I first laid eyes on him, I admit I was only sexually attracted to him. But overtime there was something about him that made me want him to be around forever. When I found out I was pregnant, I knew I would have to eventually get married, but he had some work to do.

I am not the type to judge anyone, but I learned that Harris had a history of preying on weak women. He has me mistaken if he thought I would put up with even half of the shit he brings to those other women. Then the nerve of him breaking things off with me and moving on. I feel like he just threw me away. Talking about co-parenting in peace, he will fuck around and be a single parent fucking with me. And did he forget that my family is the reason why he is making more money. We saved him from a shallow grave and gave him a better life.

Abriella stood from the couch and went to Adonis's bedroom. She picked him up gently and placed him inside the car seat. After securing him, she picked up the seat then grabbed his diaper bag before exiting the bedroom. She set the alarm, exited the house, and got inside the car. She drove to Pax and Carlita's house less than five minutes away.

When she parked in the driveway, she noticed a familiar car. It was Adamo, one of the major distributors in California and her first love. Abriella felt butterflies in her stomach as she exited the car. She unlocked Adonis from the seat before grabbing the bag and going inside. When she entered, Carlita met her at the door. She grabbed Adonis and began smothering him with kisses causing him to wake up. Abriella greeted Carlita briefly and went straight to Pax's office where he was discussing business with Adamo.

Before entering, Abriella checked herself in the mirror hanging in the hall. When she opened the door, Pax and Adamo were in deep conversation and smoking cigars. When Adamo saw Abriella, he stood to his feet and greeted her with a warm hug and kiss on the forehead. He excused himself to allow

Abriella and Pax privacy. As soon as he was out the room, she wasted no time discussing her issue with Pax.

"I think we should consider finding a replacement for Harris," said Abriella, taking a seat.

Pax gave her a questioning look and gestured for her to continue.

"He has too much baggage and since we are not getting married, he does not need to be connected with our family anymore."

"Abriella, what does that have to do with the business we have? If this baggage is not affecting my money, I see no issue," said Pax, readjusting himself in his chair.

"But, Pax, I don't want him to have any connections with our family," countered Abriella.

"Abriella, Harris is already connected to our family. Did you forget you have a son with him? So even if I wanted to break ties with him, I would still have to consider the fact that he is the father of Adonis. And let's be clear, I chose Harris for my business, not to fuck my niece and impregnate her. But I can't blame him, you are a very attractive woman that threw yourself at him."

Pax leaned into the desk and continued, "Besides, Harris does great business and has not harmed you in anyway physically. So why I would stop my money from flowing over some pussy? Abriella, you are clearly not thinking straight. It seems like your emotions are tied into the decision to handle business and survive."

Abriella spilled tears of anger. She knew her uncle was raw, but she had never heard him speak in such a manner to her. She took a few minutes to get herself together. "You're right, money over everything. I will figure it out and be careful not to disturb your wonderful business relationship," she spoke, now standing up and getting herself together. She proceeded to leave the room, but Pax stopped her.

"Abriella, if the goal is to have a husband and family then Adamo is still very much interested in you. He has expressed and demonstrated the same relationship goals you are trying to force from Harris. Now, the only thing is that Adamo's family is serious about their bloodline and don't accept outside children. Maybe Adamo is changing that because he is still very much interested in you."

Abriella exited the office without responding. She went straight to one of the bedrooms and laid on the bed. She began thinking about what Pax said and how she would move forward. She had conquered everything she set out to do but have a husband. Now in her mid-thirties, the clock was ticking. She had spent most of her life learning the game from her uncle and could run his business just like him, so she was a great asset.

Carlita entered the room with Adonis and spoke, "I knew when you started a relationship with Harris that we would come to the moment of love verses money. Abriella, for you to be in a happy relationship, you need to focus on love and family only and not the business. I am pretty sure that you were driving Harris to be perfect based on your unrealistic standards. When you decided to pursue him, you didn't take the time to get to know him enough before giving him a son. Now you are seeing the belly of the beast. I heard you requesting Pax to stop doing business with Harris because of your emotions. Now is that something you would normally do? Because as long as I have known you, you have never allowed your emotions to tamper with your business decisions."

Abriella set up on the bed and wiped the tears before opening her arms to receive Adonis.

"Abriella, if your goal is having a husband then Adamo is staying for dinner tonight. You may want to freshen up and join us in a couple hours," finished Carlita before leaving the room.

Abriella kissed Adonis before feeding and changing him. She then freshened up for dinner. She was going to put her game face on and move on from Harris and find happiness.

Kansas City

Rayvin parked in front of the nursing home. She exited the car, made her way to the entrance, then pushed the buzzer. When the clerk let her in, she approached the desk and requested her mother's room number.

Rayvin knew for the past two years that her mother's health was declining. She was too angry to see about her but lately she was having a change of heart. She felt the need to connect with her. Kyle, her uncle, who was the only family member she communicated with, informed her that her mother was gravely ill, and her days were numbered.

Rayvin walked down the hall thinking about the moment she would lay eyes on her mother. She was nervous, only remembering the last time she saw her was when she was yelling for her to get out. Her heart pounded loud like drums when she reached room 411. She entered the room to find her mother laying in a bed behind the curtain.

When she came around the curtain, she gasped at the sight of her mother unconscious with various medical equipment hooked up to her. She walked over to the bed and her mother opened her eyes. She was not able to talk but her eyes told Rayvin she was sorry.

Suddenly, her mother took one last breath and died. Rayvin stood back as staff entered. The nurses removed all equipment and cleaned her mother up before exiting the room leaving Rayvin alone again. She took a seat across the room and just looked at her mother. She tried to remember the good times she had with her as a child but there was not many. She wondered why she felt so hurt about her mother dying and why she needed to reconnect with her. Her thoughts were disturbed by her phone vibrating, it was Harris. He knew she was planning to see her mother and was calling to check on her, but Rayvin decided to not take the call.

"Are you okay, niece?" spoke Kyle, entering the room.

"Yes, I am fine, I see death all the time," responded Rayvin, never taking her eyes off her mother.

"I understand you see death all the time but witnessing your mother die is a totally different thing," said Kyle.

"Uncle Kyle, I don't know why you are asking that bitch anything. She does not care about this family," said a male voice. When Rayvin looked up, her cousin Benson was standing next to Kyle.

"The only person in this family that gave a fuck about me was Uncle Kyle!" yelled Rayvin. She walked over to Benson and stood in front of him, matching his evil stare.

"You two calm down, this is not the place or time for this type of behavior," said Kyle.

"You're right, Uncle Kyle. Another place and another time," said Benson, backing away from Rayvin.

"You know what, just send me the funeral information and I will attend," said Rayvin, preparing to leave the room.

"You can't disappear on me, you have to wait for the lawyer to read the will," said Kyle.

"No, I don't, momma would have never left me anything," said Rayvin.

"You were her only child left so why wouldn't she," said Kyle. He gave her a piece of paper with an address, date, and time written on it.

Rayvin took the paper and left the room.

"Uncle Kyle, why you trusting that bitch? She is the reason why Josh, Ricky, and Treavor are dead," said Benson.

"How do you know that?" questioned Kyle.

"Because that nigga Cameron told me before he died," responded Benson.

"Well Cameron is not a reliable source, you see what he did to his own friend," said Kyle before leaving the room. He went to the nurses' station and gave information on what funeral home would be picking up his sister's body.

In the parking lot, Rayvin sat inside her car contemplating whether she was going to kill her cousin Benson now or later. When she saw him exit the front doors, they made eye contact as he walked to his car.

He held his shirt up displaying his gun before yelling, "I'm always ready to get down, you snake ass bitch!"

Rayvin gritted her teeth and clutched her gun. It would be easy to just shoot it out with her cousin right now, but when her Uncle Kyle exited the building, she decided not to act. Instead, she started her engine and sped out the parking lot.

After dinner, Abriella and Adamo sat on the beach enjoying a bottle of red wine. It had been a long time since she was able to spend time with a man after giving birth to Adonis. She was happy to have a distraction from Harris and looking forward to a romantic evening.

"Your son is adorable. Where is his father?" questioned Adamo.

"He lives here in Florida. We decided to co-parent. He was not husband material," responded Abriella, taking a sip of her wine.

"I am not surprised you said that for two reasons. One, you aim for perfection so it's hard to please you. Two, I am the only man in this universe that can make you happy," spoke Adamo with confidence.

"You know, you may be right. I mean why did we go our separate ways?" questioned Abriella.

"I know exactly why. You were not ready to retire from the business and move to California with me," responded Adamo.

"Look, don't criticize me for having high standards and thinking about money first. During that time, I was trying to gain the respect of many. It's hard for a woman in this business. But now that the respect has been earned and I am not viewed as weak, I am ready to settle down and start a family," said Abriella.

"That's interesting, but why did you not come seek me when you were ready? You know you have my heart so why would you go and have a child with another man. Then I learn that you did not require him to marry you before you gave him a son. The baby that was supposed to be mines. And now the relationship is over, and your child is not even one years old yet," spoke Adamo. His words stung but Abriella concealed how defensive she was.

Adamo could tell he struck and nerve and continued,

"Look, you are my true love and I have been waiting for you to be ready for the love I have to give. If you still want that dream, I am here for it. However, there is only one thing you will have to do for us to be together."

"What is it?" questioned Abriella, refilling her glass with wine.

"Only you can come, not Adonis," answered Adamo.

"Yeah, your family tradition," said Abriella, now sobering up.

She took a drink of her wine and looked out onto the dark water as the full moon beamed over the ocean. The proposition made her think about her mother and how she abandoned her and her father to go marry and start a new life. She was hurt by that, but her father, Uncle Pax, and Aunt Carlita gave her so much love, her mother leaving never impacted her. Now she found herself in the same situation and felt guilty that she was actually thinking about it instead of smacking Adamo and leaving him on the beach.

"The fact that you have not slapped me and barged away means that you are contemplating. Take some time to think about it but don't take too long. My father is ready for grandchildren, and I intend to honor his wishes very soon. I will be here for another week. If you decide before then, we can go back to California and plan the most glamorous wedding. If you can't make up your mind that fast then I will be in California, and you know how to find me. Just don't leave me waiting too long."

He gave Abriella a kiss on the lips and stood up before heading back to the house and retreated to the guest bedroom to get some sleep. For the next few hours, Abriella sat in the sand thinking about everything. She loved Adonis but the reality was that she would be raising him alone without a husband and that was not perfect. She hated that she brought an innocent child in the world and would not be able to give him what he deserved. She thought about Harris and how good of a father he seemed to his other children. She had to admit, even though his family was complicated, their children received love and knew what unity was. She knew that if she died at this very moment, Adonis would be in good hands.

She had to stop and wonder if her mother sat like this before making the decision to abandon her. Suddenly, her thoughts were disturbed by Carlita who took a seat next to her.

"So how did your night go with Adamo? He seems happy," spoke Carlita.

"He wants to marry me, and I would never want for anything ever again. But he wants me to retire, and Adonis can't come," responded Abriella.

"Wow! His family still holding that tradition? You would think that it would be extinct after decades. Abriella, the way you are sitting out here makes me think you are considering it."

When Abriella did not respond, Carlita cradled her face and gently turned it to face hers before speaking, "Abriella, you are not considering doing what you mother did to you are you? Please don't do that. You are a strong woman that has broken many cycles. You persevered despite the fact your mother abandoned you. You learned your uncle's business and would be the one to carry on his legacy. You are one of the first woman to run things. And you mean to tell me that you are really sitting here thinking about abandoning Adonis! My God if I knew that damn tradition was still thriving, I would have put you out before dinner."

When Abriella still didn't respond, Carlita threw her hands up and continued,

"You know when your mother left you with your father, it was a blessing in disguise for me. I could not understand how a mother could leave their child. As for myself, I made the decision not to have children because I chose business instead of being a mother. But the years I spent with you as a child made me regret that. When you had Adonis, I was so proud of you for choosing to be a mother. But now I am sitting here shocked that you are considering this."

Upset, Carlita hurried to the house and retreated to the nursery where Adonis was sleeping.

Abriella grabbed the wine glasses, wine bottle, and went inside. She cleaned the glasses and threw the empty bottle in the trash before going to the nursery to find Carlita standing over the crib crying. She ignored her auntie while grabbing her son and his diaper bag before leaving the house and heading home. It bothered her that her aunt was upset with her, but it did not change the fact that she was still considering going to be with Adamo. When she made it home, she entered the house and put her son in the crib before going to the kitchen and opening another bottle of wine. She sat on her couch and drank wine as she listened to Anita Baker while thinking.

No matter how upset her aunt was she still could not say no to the idea of moving to California living happily ever after. Her uncle knew about the tradition and placed it in her hands and that meant that whatever decision she made, he would not turn his back on her.

At home, Pax sat up in bed reading a Forbes magazine while Carlita sat at her vanity brushing her long salt and pepper hair. Pax peeked over the magazine, catching a glimpse. He could tell Carlita was upset about something.

"Is everything okay, honey? You seem upset," he questioned.

"Did you know that Adamo's family still holds that crazy tradition about their bloodline?" questioned Carlita, turning around to face him.

"Yes, I had an idea but was not sure if Adamo was still carrying it on because he still pursued Abriella even after knowing she had a son. But I warned Abriella about that," said Pax.

"So, you gave her a blessing to abandon her son," Carlita spat.

"I wasn't giving her a blessing but considering her desire. You know the desire you had to run the business instead of having children," said Pax.

"Oh, so this is about me not giving you children! How many times do I have to apologize for that!" yelled Carlita, bursting into tears.

"I am not punishing you for it anymore, but it was only when my brother died, and we took in Abriella that I was able to forgive and move on. You being the head of a business and watching Abriella conquer so much opened my mind to the fact that some sacrifices may look and sound grim but are necessary. I spent a lot of time trying to get over the fact that my love for you was stronger than continuing my bloodline. So, if Abriella decides to follow her desire, then Adonis has plenty of family that will love him."

Carlita slammed her brush on the vanity and exited the bedroom. She knew that if she stayed in the room with her husband with so many emotions, she would probably say or do something she would regret. She went to the kitchen and retrieved a bottle of tequila and a shot glass before going to the deck and sitting down. She took shots until she could no longer focus straight before passing out.

Hours later, Pax awakened to find she never came to bed. He got up and walked around the house until he found her outside snoring on the deck. It was now 6:00am as he awakened her and helped her to the bedroom to bed.

On the way to Atlanta, Harris stopped in North Carolina to pick up Tameka and Karris. They would travel to drop his daughters off and possibly see the new baby if he felt up to it. When Tameka entered the car, everyone was in the backseat asleep.

"Karris, be quiet until your sisters wake up," instructed Tameka, giving her some headphones and her iPad. Once Karris was settled, Tameka put on her seat belt and looked over at Harris.

"Damn, you look like a hermit. But I heard you are doing quite well, the kids are giving good reports," said Tameka.

Harris smiled then placed the SUV in drive. They road in silence for several minutes before Tameka spoke again, "How are things going with Abriella? I know it's a sore subject, but we always have discussed the hard things?"

When Tameka insisted on riding to Atlanta, Harris was relieved because he needed her so he could really vent. They had both seen each other in their vulnerable states so he could always tell her anything.

"We are officially done, and she agrees to co-parent," said Harris.

"I am not surprised. When I met her at Bennie's, she seemed so disconnected from everything. It is like everything in her world is a business transaction," said Tameka.

"You are right! She had all these rules and regulations on how she needed me to be after she fucked the shit out of me and let me get her pregnant. When I moved on my own and started focusing on myself, I began to fall out of love with her. Now I didn't plan on leaving her, I was willing to sacrifice and marry her just for my son. But when I dropped Adonis off this last time, I just could not take it anymore. My peace of mind and happiness is important."

"Well, whatever happens in your world, just know I am proud of you because you really bossed up instead of going crazy like we were afraid of. And your father is who! Now I can't believe Cassandra didn't tell me that," said Tameka.

"Yeah, that's a whole other thing. She has not been answering my calls because she knows it's time to explain. Uncle Bennie said it's a touchy subject and to lay off. But fuck that shit, I want to know why from her mouth, and then I am done with it," spoke Harris.

"Well, just be careful with her. You don't want to do anything that would send her spiraling back into the world of addiction. The way I see it, that shit was probably so painful that she suppresses it. You know in our generation that's what our parents did to us. They never allowed us to question, when shit happened it just happened, and we had to move on. For her to never want to discuss your father must be something that fucked her head up that she does not feel strong enough to revisit it. So just be easy with my mom's, you know I will beat you up about that one," finished Tameka, giving Harris a playful punch in the arm.

Harris turned up the radio and Tameka got comfortable in her seat and began listening to her audio book, "Loyal Snakes" by Rosa James.

In Kansas City, Benson sat in the interrogation room eating a double burger with cheese and bacon, large fries, and a strawberry soda, you know a meal fit for a snitch. The detectives watched him enjoy his meal for several minutes before becoming impatient.

"Mr. Davis, are you ready to tell us what we need to know?" questioned one of the detectives, losing his patience.

Benson took a drink of his soda while chewing and swallowed. He took another bite before talking with his mouth full, allowing small particles of food to fall onto the steel table, "So, the nigga Cameron told me that Harris and his Uncle

Bennie killed my cousins back in the day. There's no statute of limitation on murder, right?" spoke Benson, grabbing a fry.

"No, there is no statute of limitation, however, we can't use a dead man's words coming from a convicted felon and child molester to stand up in court," said the female detective.

"You right about that, what type of evidence do you need?" questioned Benson.

"Look, the murder case is cold as ice, but do you know anything about the drugs? We have been trying to get the Grimes family for years and nothing holds up. If you can get us something that sticks and can hold up in court, then you can receive your money," said the male detective.

"Don't worry, I got you! I know someone that runs close with Harris and his uncle," said Benson before getting up and exiting the room, leaving the mess on the table.

Once he was out the room, the detectives looked at each other and sighed.

"So, we just bought him a meal for nothing," spat the female detective before leaving the room and slamming the door.

CHAPTER FIFTEEN

FIX MY LIFE

Kyle parked in the back of the law firm where no one could see him. He turned off the engine and looked around until he saw the familiar car drive in the lot parking next to him.

May's father, Rufus, turned the engine off and stepped outside the Jaguar. Next, he got inside the passenger seat of Kyle's car.

"Everything should go in your favor today. I talked with the lawyer, he owes me one," said Rufus.

"Good. Then once I receive the inheritance, I can go into the sunset. Jamaica here I come," said Kyle.

He was with his sister when she made the will and knew that she was giving everything to her only living child Rayvin. Kyle played it cool but was disappointed that his sister would not consider him, the person that had always been there for her. She gave him a copy of the will and from the time he laid his eyes on the one-million-dollar policy, he had been scheming on how to get the money. He checked his watch, it was 11:00am and the meeting would start in a half hour.

"So will I see you later on this evening after your victory?" questioned Rufus, placing his hand on Kyle's thigh.

Kyle looked over at Rufus and gave him a devious smile. "I can do you one better, how about once the check clears, you meet me at the airport, and we can run away together. We have been having this secret affair for years and it's time for us to step out of the darkness and live happily ever after."

"You are right, but that check is going to take a few days to clear, and I want you right now," said Rufus, unzipping his pants releasing his manhood.

"I knew you would find a way to keep me occupied for the next twenty minutes," spoke Kyle before going down on him.

In front of the law firm, Rayvin parked and got out the car. She looked around not seeing her Uncle Kyle's car. When she entered the office building, the secretary escorted her to the conference room for the meeting. When the lawyer saw Rayvin, he swallowed hard not sure how she would react to the reading of the altered will. Rayvin took a seat not sure why her presence was requested in the first place. She and the lawyer sat quietly for the next ten minutes before Kyle entered. He greets his niece with a hug and shook the lawyer's hand before taking a seat.

"Okay, let's get on with it, this should be quick, "said the attorney and began to read.

"This is the last will and testament of Cathy Ruthann Williams. I, Cathy Ruthann Williams, will my entire estate, property, and finances to my brother, Kyle Williams."

He retrieved two envelopes from the folder and handed one to Rayvin and the other to her uncle. Kyle was so curious about what was in Rayvin's envelope, he did not bother to open his own. Rayvin looked at the envelope before looking at the attorney.

"Are we done here? I have things to do," she spoke, standing up from her chair.

"We are if you don't have any questions," answered the attorney, now feeling guilty.

Rayvin gave her uncle a brief hug before leaving the office and exiting the building. She wasn't looking forward to anything from her mother and was frustrated that the attorney wasted her time. She would rather be in Atlanta seeing Daisy's new baby or in California with Toni, Cassandra, and Destiny. She entered the car in time to see her uncle exit the building and for some reason, she wondered what was in the envelope he had. Remembering she had an envelope she opened it and began reading the letter.

Dear Rayvin, I just want to let you know that I love you and I am sorry for not being the mother you needed. I wish we had an opportunity to mend our relationship but when I was diagnosed with lung cancer and then caught Covid 19, I knew my days were numbered and I had to make sure you knew that I was sorry and love you. Your Uncle Kyle has been taking care of me, but I am sure he is expecting something out of it. This is off the subject, but did you know that he was having an affair with Rufus Adams? Isn't that Harris's son's grandfather. I thought I would let you know, because he started hanging around more often after I took out a life insurance policy for one million dollars. The money is yours. I know it can't fill the void, but it's the only thing I could do to show you I am sorry since time is running out. I love you, Rayvin. I am sorry. Until we meet again, your mother.

Rayvin sat staring at the letter, thinking about the meeting with the attorney. She had to admit the attorney seemed off and Kyle was not as caring as usual. She had money but the fact that she was being cheated had her thinking. Her thoughts were disturbed by someone tapping on her window. When she looked, it was her uncle. He could not see her through the presidential tint as she placed the letter inside the console before rolling the window down.

"Are you okay, niece? You left so fast and now you are just sitting out here," said Kyle, looking around to see if he could spot the envelope.

"Oh, I am fine, I just read that letter from mother in the bathroom and had a moment," Rayvin lied.

"Well, I am sure your mother meant every word she said in the letter. And if you need anything, just let me know. But I am confused on why she left me everything instead of her only living child," said Kyle.

His statement made Rayvin angry, but she kept her cool instead of grabbing her gun and shooting him at close range.

"It can't bother me if it's something I never expected. Besides, money has never been an issue for me," responded Rayvin, starting her car.

"Want to join me for dinner later?" questioned Kyle.

"No, I need to get some rest. I have to fly to Virginia to visit a friend, then I must get back for mother's services," Rayvin lied, placing her car in drive.

Kyle stood back and watched her drive away. He headed to his car glad that Rayvin was not pitching a fuss about not being willed anything.

In the car, Rayvin changed her mind about going to Atlanta. She dialed Harris to let him know that she was not going to come until after the funeral. When he answered, she spoke, "Hey, so I am going to stick around in the city until after mom's funeral. There's something going on I need to see about."

"What's going on? I need details?" questioned Harris, relaxing on the hotel bed.

"Shit where do I start. So, the reading of the will was bullshit. She gave Kyle everything, so I am not sure why my presence was requested. Then my mother writes me a heartfelt letter apologizing and told me that she left me money. But the most important thing that I need you to know is that your almost father-in-law Rufus is on the DL with my Uncle Kyle. My mother said he started hanging around more after she took a life insurance policy out for one million dollars."

"What! Rufus on the down low! That shit would have fucked May's ass up," said Harris.

"I know, shit is always crazy in Kansas City. But I also have a feeling that my mother was warning me about Kyle," said Rayvin.

"Shit your feeling is right! You know how you can find out! Go to May's mother June with this information. She is all about her image and will do anything to protect her husband being on the down low. Give me a few hours, I will be up there, you don't have to deal with this alone." He ended the call.

He went online and booked a fight to Kansas City before taking a shower and preparing for an early dinner with Daisy and Lewis. When he arrived in Atlanta, he had Tameka drop him off at the hotel before going to Daisy's. Just then he received a text message from Lewis confirming his presence to dinner. When Harris read the text, he had to respect Lewis for stepping up. He was surprised that he was not angry or jealous and that was confirmation that he had changed for the better. When his phone rung, he tossed himself on the bed before answering.

"Hey, nephew! We need to talk about some things. Are you at Daisy's?" questioned Bennie.

"I'm in Atlanta and plan to be at Daisy's for dinner," responded Harris.

"We here as well. Got an invite from Lewis. But we need to talk about this matter now," said Bennie.

"Okay, I am at the St. Regis."

"Cool, I am going to drop Effie and the boys at Daisy's and then I will come to you. We can ride back to Daisy's together." Bennie ended the call.

Harris went to the bathroom and showered before getting dressed. He sat having a drink until Bennie arrived. When he opened the door, his uncle greeted him before going straight to the bar and pouring himself a drink. He took his glass and took a seat on the couch.

"I got an interesting call today from Detective Alson. He said that Rayvin has a cousin name Benson who came in trying to snitch about Rayvin's brothers murder, talking about Cameron told him everything. Don't worry, I set that shit up to where that can't be traced back to us, but it was the fact that Benson said he could get them more information about us. That worries me because there is no telling what Cameron told him. I have a flight to Kansas City after dinner, I'm going to lay this nigga down," said Bennie before taking a drink.

"That nigga Benson, man the last time I heard about him he went to jail for molesting a little girl. But check this out. Rayvin called me about her mother's will. She said that her mother wrote her a letter and said that Kyle was having an affair with May's father. She also said her mother willed her some money but at the reading of the will, her mother gave Kyle everything."

"Bullshit, you know May's family know people in high ass places. I am surprised that June didn't find a way to get

Junior. So, I assume you heading to Kansas City after this dinner," said Bennie.

"Flight already booked," responded Harris.

"Good, we are on the same page. Now how are you feeling? I know you and Daisy was always close. Tell me how you are feeling about the new baby and fiancé," said Bennie.

"I feel complex because this is a new thing. But I am happy for her and glad to see she and the girls are happy. I give Lewis his props for standing by her. I respect how he reached out to me about the dinner and meeting the baby," said Harris.

Bennie nodded in approval. His nephew had matured and was humble. They spent the next couple hours chilling and talking before heading over to Daisy's for dinner.

Dinner at Daisy's

When Bennie parked in front of Daisy's house, he looked over at his nephew. "You ready to let her go, right?" When Harris nodded, he turned the engine off and they exited the car.

Harris followed his uncle up the cobblestone walkway. As he got closer to the house, he began feeling lightheaded. Bennie turned around and asked if he was okay. When Harris nodded, he continued to the front door. Before he could knock, Lewis opened the door welcoming them inside.

"Great timing, I just took the steaks off the grill," said Lewis, holding the door open inviting them inside.

"Daisy and Tameka are in the kitchen preparing the food for the table, so we have time for a drink in my mancave," continued Lewis, gesturing for Harris and Bennie to follow.

"A mancave? That's what I am talking about," said Bennie, patting Harris on the back.

The men went down to the lower level and Lewis turned on the lights before heading to the bar. "Feel free to take a seat and get comfortable," spoke Lewis, retrieving three glasses and the ice bucket from the freezer.

Harris took a seat as Bennie walked around admiring the decoration. "I see you still down with the Kansas City Chiefs and Royals," said Bennie.

"Until the day I die," responded Lewis, handing Harris and Bennie their drinks before retrieving his. He took a seat across from them. "Harris, thanks for taking my invite and coming. Now that I am a father, I understand how important it is to know who my children will be around. I have been around your children for a long time, and I just want you to get to know me, so you won't be uncomfortable."

"Man, I can respect that," responded Bennie, looking over at Harris.

Everyone took a drink and tried to deal with the awkward silence that followed for several seconds. Harris knew it was his turn to talk but he felt scrambled. He and Daisy had been in a complicated relationship for years and now it was officially time to accept that another man would be taking his place. He opened his mouth to speak hoping that the words that followed would not be full of malice,

"Lewis, thanks for inviting me. I respect a man that step up to the plate and understand how important it is to become acquainted with Daisy's family. I know we had a complicated history, but the fact that you are here today speaks in volumes. I know you love Daisy and my daughters; the girls talk about you all the time. Congratulations on your son, it's such a joy to have children and Daisy is a wonderful mother."

Bennie nodded at Harris giving him confirmation that he was doing great.

"So would you like to meet my son?" questioned Lewis, finishing his drink.

Bennie and Harris finished their drinks and followed Lewis to the nursery. When they entered, Bennie and Harris went into the private bathroom and washed their hands.

"Wow, I never thought I would be here today doing this," said Bennie in a low voice, drying his hands.

"Tell me about it, this feels awkward but it's our reality," said Harris before exiting the restroom.

Lewis was standing by the crib, holding the baby. He turned and smiled before handing him Harris. "Meet Malachi Lewis Anderson," spoke Lewis.

Harris looked down at the sleeping baby and all he could see was himself. He shook his thoughts thinking that it was just him tripping. But when he saw the identical birthmark behind the baby's left ear, he gasped and handed the baby to Bennie. He stood in silence and waited for his uncle to catch the same thing.

When Bennie saw the birthmark, he looked up at Lewis then back at Harris before speaking, "Damn, Malachi has the same birthmark as Harris. What a coincidence." He handed the baby back to Lewis.

Daisy walked in the room with a worried look on her face. "Hey, I was looking all over for you guys. We are at the table hungry and waiting," she spoke, retrieving her baby from Lewis and leaving the room.

The men followed Daisy down the hall to the dining area before taking their seats. Lewis led grace and everyone began eating. Harris sat quietly eating as he calculated the timeframe that he and Daisy slept together. He did it twice to make sure and the numbers were adding up that he was the father.

Bennie lost his appetite; he knew that the baby was a part of his bloodline. Effie could sense something was wrong with her husband, so she placed her hand on his and gave him a concerned look.

"Daisy, you have a beautiful son," spoke Harris, cutting another piece of the steak.

"Thank you, Harris. He is so dear to me. I never thought I would ever have children again especially a bouncing baby boy," responded Daisy.

"That's wonderful! So, when are you going to tell me that I am his father?" said Harris, dropping his fork and knife.

The children began looking back and forth at each other whispering. Bennie cradled his head and sighed.

"Okay, kids, let's give the grownups some time," said Tameka. She retrieved Malachi from the swing and followed Effie and the children out of the dining area.

When the coast was clear, Harris continued, "Look, Daisy, I understand that you are moving on. But not telling me that this baby is my son is a problem. Then Lewis walking around talking about this is his son. What type of games are you playing?" questioned Harris.

Daisy began to cry. She knew the birthmark was a dead giveaway but hoped no one made a big deal out of it.

"Would you guys like for me to leave the room?" questioned Lewis.

"No, Lewis you have a right to be here," responded Bennie.

Frustrated, Daisy slammed her fist on the table before speaking, "Fuck, Harris, I know he is your son. I was trying to move on with my life and then found out I was pregnant. I am tired and want to settle down and have a good life. I fell in love with Lewis, and I want to be with him. When I saw that pregnancy test, I was like, damn, 'God are you going to keep me in this emotional roller coaster with Harris for the rest of my life?' I love you like family, but I felt that if I would have told you this was your son then you would not have accepted that I wanted to still be with Lewis."

Harris took a moment to process her words. "I can see why you would think that I am trying to trap you. I wasted a lot of your time keeping you in my vicious web. But when we slept together that night in May's house, we were both drunk and vulnerable and just trying to make the situation feel good. If I was not going to accept you moving on, I would have made it a problem with my girls being around Lewis. Daisy, I have every right to know my son and I am sitting here to assure you that I am okay with releasing you. But I need to be in my son's life."

Daisy began to cry. Bennie stood up and went over to her and gave her a hug, reassuring her that it would be okay. Harris looked over at Lewis who was focused on Daisy.

"Hey, Lewis, I am good if you are good. I understand that you look at him like a son as well and I am willing to share that with you," spoke Harris.

Lewis smiled and reached over the table to shake Harris's hand. "Don't worry, your children are in good hands with me," Lewis spoke.

Harris went over to Daisy and gave her a hug. "You are always my family and I want you to be happy," said Harris.

"Well, that's all settled. I hate to end such a touching moment, but my nephew and I must prepare for a flight. And, Daisy, you knew damn well you were not about to get that off especially with the birthmark! All due respect for your father, you should change the baby's name to Kacey," said Bennie before laughing, trying to lighten up the situation.

"Bennie, why you always cracking jokes at the worst time," said Daisy, laughing as she wiped her tears with the napkin.

Everyone shared a laugh and went to the den where Effie, Tameka, and the children were talking. Bennie and Harris said their goodbye's before leaving to go to the airport to catch their flights to Kansas City. While driving, Bennie exited the freeway.

When Harris gave him a questioning, look Bennie spoke, "No worries, nephew, I changed the flights to late tomorrow morning. Look, I have been shacked up, parenting, was shot, had to stay in a rehab to get back on track. All I want to do is see some random ass, drink Hennessy out the bottle, and shoot ones out of that money gun in VIP, so are you down or what?"

"Hell, yeah, I am down for some random ass shaking and liquor," responded Harris.

Bennie directed his GPS to Magic City.

Rayvin and June

In Kansas City, Rayvin sat a half a block away from May's parents' house. It was well past midnight when May's father Rufus exited the garage and drove down the street. Rayvin waited another half hour before going to the front door and knocking. She observed the bedroom light come on and moments later, June opened the door.

When June saw Rayvin, she displayed a look of confusion. "It's late. Is everything okay with Junior?"

"We need to talk. In fact, I need you to put something on quick and ride with me. I have something to show you about your husband," spoke Rayvin before turning to walk away.

"Look, Rayvin, I am not new to this, I know my husband hangs out late and cheats. So, if this is what you are here about then don't bother to waste my time," responded June.

She proceeded to close the door, but Rayvin used her foot to block it. "But do you know who he is cheating with?" Rayvin questioned.

June gave Rayvin a stern look and invited her inside while she went upstairs to get dressed. Ten minutes later, she came downstairs wearing a navy blue sweatsuit and tennis shoes. They exited the house and went to Rayvin's car that was now parked out front. They road in silence, heading to the Sheraton Hotel in the plaza area.

"Been seeing this hotel on the credit card statements a lot," said June, exiting the car.

They went inside where Rayvin approached the clerk who slid her two key cards. Rayvin handed June the one to the room Rufus was inside of while keeping the key to the hotel room next door.

"Your husband is in room number 365, I have room 364 reserved if you need a moment before going in," said Rayvin.

June didn't respond as she turned and went to the elevator. Rayvin followed behind and they road up to the 3rd floor. June got off the elevator and walked down the hall at a fast pace. When she reached the hotel room door, she stopped and look at Rayvin who was entering the room next door.

"Wait! I need a minute," said June, rushing past Rayvin into the room. She took a seat on one of the double beds and looked up at Rayvin. "Why are you showing me this? I have not been very kind to your family so there has to be something you want in return."

Rayvin responded, "Your husband is in the room with the person that is trying to steal the inheritance that's due to me from my mother. She wrote me a letter before she died and told me about your husband's affair and that he may be involved in pulling some strings to alter the will."

"And if I don't help you what will happen?" questioned June.

Rayvin smiled before speaking, "Then the whole Kansas City will know your husband's dirty secret. This won't be no simple cheating scandal. This will not only tarnish your marriage but change the way you look at your husband along with everyone else."

June took a deep breath before standing up and walking over to the door. She placed her hand on the knob and turned to Rayvin. "You wait for me, because I will definitely need a ride home," she spoke before exiting.

She went to room 365 and swiped the key card. She opened the door slowly and eased inside. The sight of her husband bent over having sex with another man took her breath. The men were so engrossed in their sexual escapade, they never noticed June. She backed into the shadows and watched for a few minutes trying to process what she was seeing. Tears drained from her eyes as she kept pinching herself to make sure it was not a nightmare. When she could no longer take it, she crept out the hotel room.

Rayvin had the door ajar waiting for her to return. When June walked in, the pain and humiliation was written all over her face. Rayvin handed her one of the shots from the bar of scotch and watched June guzzle it down before retrieving another one.

"Look, I am sorry I had to show you this," said Rayvin, now feeling remorse.

"No, you're not! But don't worry about me because I will be okay," responded June.

"No, I am truly sorry. But I would have still done this to get my money," said Rayvin.

"That's sound more genuine. Can we stay here? I want to see how long he stays with this man," said June.

When Rayvin nodded, June continued,

"When I married Rufus, I was already pregnant with May. My parents would have killed me if they knew that I was pregnant by someone else because it was all about protecting the family image. Rufus knew that May was not his child, but we got married anyway to please everyone and for financial stability. I felt like I owed him a favor for marrying me while carrying another man's child. The stipulations were that I had children with him. But for some reason, God would not allow us to create a child together. Rufus began to resent me after years of trying. When I found out he was cheating, he used our issues with conceiving a child as an excuse to why he was doing it, so I gave him a pass."

June stopped talking and began staring off into space for several seconds. Rayvin, who was laying comfortable in the other bed, tossed her another shot of scotch. When the bottle landed on June's lap, she snapped out of her trance, opened the bottle of scotch, and took a drink.

"This is why God would not allow me to get pregnant again. Then my only child watched me stay in a miserable marriage for her and she ended up trying to salvage a relationship with her son's father. Talk about vicious cycles. She was only doing what she saw at home. But you know what, this shit stops today. So, Rayvin, we have all night. Now it's time for you to tell me your story."

Rayvin went to the mini bar and grabbed the rest of the shots of liquor. She sat on the bed next to June and opened her drink. "The man in the room is Kyle, my uncle. He took care of my mother when she became ill. My mother and I have not talked since I was seventeen years old. But she wrote me this letter apologizing. I want what my mother gave me because she has never given me anything in this life but bringing me into this world to fend for myself."

For the first time in years, Rayvin allowed herself to cry for her mother. June wrapped her arms around her and began rocking while humming the song she used to hum to May when she needed someone to hold and comfort her. Rayvin melted into June's nurturing embrace for several minutes. She could never remember being held by her mother and it felt good. She ended up falling asleep. When she awakened, hours had passed, and June was in the bathroom brushing her teeth and getting dressed.

"Why didn't you wake me! Are they still inside the room?" questioned Rayvin.

"No, they left two hours ago so I followed them. When I saw they were having breakfast together, I hurried home to grab some things, made some calls, and we need to get down to the attorney's office as soon as you get dressed. I retrieved your bag from the trunk of your car with your clothing. You think you can be ready in 30 minutes?" asked June before drinking some water to rinse her mouth.

Rayvin grabbed her bag to retrieve her clothing and hygiene products. June waited in the lobby as she enjoyed coffee and a bagel. Twenty minutes later, Rayvin came down to the lobby. They road to the law firm and June explained everything. When they entered Mr. Douglas office, June threatened to report him if he did not contact the bank and cancel the check to Kyle's account. The attorney could not give Rayvin eye contact as he sat on the phone waiting for the bank. When finished, the lawyer handed Rayvin the original check for the inheritance.

"Thank you for your help, and don't worry, I will handle Rufus," said June before standing and exiting the conference room.

When alone with Rayvin, the attorney spoke, "Rayvin, I am so sorry about—"

He was cut off by Rayvin who placed her hand up. She exited the conference room not bothering to say goodbye. When she made it to the parking lot, June was in the driver seat of her Mustang.

"Come on, honey! Let's get that check cashed so I can go home and wreck some shit!" yelled June from the car window.

Rayvin laughed and got inside the passenger seat. They sped out the parking lot to the bank.

Harris sat in the terminal next to his uncle who was asleep. They closed Magic City and went to have breakfast before going to the airport.

Harris dialed his mother's phone number and it rung several times before going to voicemail. He knew she was awake, so he tried again, determined to make her answer. While the cell rung for the second time, Cassandra sat on the deck drinking her coffee and reading the newspaper.

She ignored the second call but when it rung for the third time, she snatched her phone from the table and answered, "Good morning, son."

Harris got right to the conversation, "Uncle Bennie told me that Kevin was my father. Why couldn't you tell me this?" He spoke in a low voice. Bennie heard the name Kevin and opened one eye. When he saw that Harris was on the phone, he acted as he was still asleep while listening.

"Yes, Kevin is your father. I did not tell you because things were complicated," answered Cassandra.

"Cameron has been my brother all this time? Why did you not feel this was important for me to know? What if knowing who we really were to each other changed the outcome of things?" questioned Harris

Cassandra's hands began to shake. Just hearing Kevin's name still brought out raw emotions. She still loved him, and his rejection broke her heart beyond repair. She spent years suppressing any thought of him and was at a good point. But now her son was asking questions that she did not want to answer.

"Look, son, I just can't talk about this. You grew up with everything you wanted and needed so just please let it go," pleaded Cassandra.

"Momma! You are being selfish. What about how this new information has affected me?" countered Harris.

"How has it affected you? You would not even be asking about this if Bennie didn't run his fucking mouth and tell you about it! And while we are on the subject, what all did he tell you!" yelled Cassandra.

"He told me that Kevin broke your heart and was the reason you started doing drugs. He told me that the family fought hard for you to get on track," responded Harris.

"Sounds like he told you all you needed to know. There is nothing more to say about it," said Cassandra.

"You know what, momma, you are right. I just wanted to see if you were going to tell me your side. I am on my way to Kansas City to support Rayvin. And while I am there, I plan to find Kevin and talk to him and hear his side," said Harris before ending the call.

Cassandra sat the phone back on the table and began to cry. She didn't want to revisit any thoughts of Kevin and was angry with Bennie for telling Harris about him. When Destiny came outside onto the balcony, Cassandra hurried and wiped her tears.

"Grandma, everyone has gone to see Daisy's new baby but us, when can we go?" questioned Destiny, showing her a photo of the baby that Clarise texted her.

When Cassandra looked at the photo of Malachi, she knew the baby belonged to Harris.

"Oh, yeah, Jamie said he has the same birthmark that I have," said Destiny, grabbing her phone.

"I bet he does! Do me a favor and call Daisy and see if you can stay with them for a few days. I will call your school and get your assignments," said Cassandra.

Once Daisy confirmed that Destiny could come, Cassandra booked the flights. She would fly to Atlanta with Destiny and visit briefly before heading to Kansas City. She did not want Harris to talk to his father without her.

Later that evening, Kevin knocked on the hotel room door and waited a few seconds before the door opened. When he entered, Twyla was standing in the middle of the room rocking the baby to sleep.

"Why did you come to Kansas City? I told you I was coming to you," spoke Kevin.

"Trust me, I was not trying to come back here but I had no choice. The bank account I put the money in is frozen and the main branch is here. I have been working to get it resolved so I can get out of this city," responded Twyla.

"Twyla, we have to get out of here. Could you book some flights to Texas?" questioned Kevin.

"No, I don't have enough money on hand. I spent money on this room for a couple more days and Cameron Jr. needs formula and pampers. I can barely buy myself a burger," said Twyla.

"Well, I am going to get out here and make some moves and get us some money so we can get out of here," said Kevin, pacing the floor.

"So, is it true? Did everyone move out of Kansas City?" inquired Twyla.

"That's what it looks like, but we still have to be careful because they have eyes and ears all over the place. You never know when one of them are in town," responded Kevin. When his phone vibrated, he frowned at the unfamiliar number. "Hello?"

"Kevin, this is Harris. I know that you are my father."

When Kevin heard those words, he allowed his body to drop into sitting position on the bed. They shared an awkward silence.

"I don't mean any harm. I just want to meet and talk with you. You pick the place and time," said Harris.

"How did you get my phone number?" questioned Kevin, looking over at Twyla.

"I have my ways, but like I said, I just want to meet with you and hear your side of the story," said Harris.

"Okay, I will contact you in a couple days with a time and place." Kevin ended the call. He stood from the bed and began pacing again.

"Who was that? Is everything okay?" questioned Twyla.

"Yes and no. Harris is not dead, and he wants to meet with me," said Kevin.

When Twyla heard that Harris was still alive, she placed the baby on the bed and began pacing the floor. She knew that once he found her, he would kill her.

"Kevin, Cameron and I was sure that we killed Harris," she spoke.

"Well, that was definitely him on the phone. He wants to meet with me to talk about some things," said Kevin.

"What could he possibly want from you other than to get to me?" questioned Twyla.

"I wish it was that simple, Twyla. You see Harris is my son," responded Kevin.

When Twyla heard those words, her knees buckled. Kevin caught her just in time before she hit the floor.

"Don't worry, I will get you the money so you and Cameron Jr. can get out of here asap. I am going to meet with him. This is a conversation we should have had a long time ago," said Kevin.

"No! I am not leaving without you! What if he kills you," responded Twyla.

"Well, if he does, I definitely deserve it, but he also deserves this discussion. I don't want you to tell anyone about me meeting with him no matter what happens." He was tired of hiding the truth and this would be his chance to right some of the wrong decisions he made over the years. He left the hotel and began walking.

The cold late February air pierced his thin jacket as he walked looking for a car to steal. When he laid eyes on a Chevy Impala, he made sure the coast was clear before breaking in and stealing the car. As he drove, he rummaged through the glove compartment trying to find anything of value that he could sale or pawn for money so that he could get Twyla and the baby to Texas.

After arriving to Kansas City earlier that day, Bennie and Harris went their separate ways.

While Harris went straight to Rayvin, who was preparing for her mother's funeral service the next day, Bennie met with his inside connection Detective Alson. The Detective was keeping tabs on Benson and was responsible for freezing Twyla's bank account. After receiving the information he needed, Bennie headed to his homie Byrd's house to get a gun, smoke some weed, and catch up. His plan was to attend Rayvin's mother's funeral service the next day and get eyes on Benson so he could follow him.

CHAPTER SIXTEEN

RAINY DAYS

When Rayvin arrived at the funeral home, Harris and Bennie were already inside sitting on the back row. When she entered the sanctuary, she made eye contact with them, giving a brief nod before heading to the front row to sit with her estranged family.

"Haven't seen Rayvin dressed up like an actual female in years," whispered Bennie, nudging Harris who shook his head while using the program to conceal his grin.

Now at the front row, Rayvin ignored the sneers from other family members as she took a seat next to Kyle. He put his arms around her. "Baby girl, you look nice. How are you holding up? Can you believe that mess with the will. I am glad they got that straightened out because I knew your mother would not just leave you nothing."

"I was surprised myself, Uncle Kyle, but you know I got you," lied Rayvin before focusing on the pastor.

He began announcing the order of service that would be short and sweet per her mother's request in the will. Rayvin knew it would piss her family off, but she didn't care and was ready for any drama anyone had to bring, especially her cousin Benson who sat on the opposite side of Kyle.

"Look at that nigga Benson sitting on the front row," whispered Harris.

"Oh, don't worry about him, he will be taken care of very soon," responded Bennie before exiting the sanctuary. He went outside to the parking lot to his car, not wanting Benson to spot him.

He knew that Benson would be at the funeral so he arrived early so he could see what type of car he was in. When he saw Benson enter and take a seat on the front row, Bennie sat in the back to keep an eye on him. The plan was to follow Benson and when the opportunity presented itself, he would kill him.

When the services were concluding, Rayvin stood up and went to the back row and sat with Harris.

"I need you to kill her today. If she is gone, then I am next in line for probate to get the money," whispered Kyle.

"I thought your peoples got that taken care of," replied Benson.

"Shit his wife found out about us and the will. I told him to keep his phone locked or delete our messages because I am sure that's how she found out about it," said Kyle.

"Okay, I got you. She will be dead before the day ends," responded Benson before standing up and walking out the sanctuary.

Outside, Harris stood with Rayvin while Bennie sat in an all-black charger behind tinted windows keeping an eye on everything. He observed Harris and Rayvin saying their goodbyes and retreating to separate cars. When he saw Benson get into a Toyota Corolla, he started his car and waited for him to pull off. When Rayvin drove out the parking lot, Benson followed. It wasn't until Bennie trailed him several blocks before he realized that Benson was following Rayvin.

"Looks like things are about to get interesting," Bennie said to himself as he turned off the car radio and his cell phone.

In the other car, Rayvin drove heading to her mother's house to make sure all the items were removed and to give a final walk through before leaving the keys inside for the landlord. She was nervous because she had never stepped foot in her mother's home since the projects. After the fifteen-minute drive, she parked in the driveway and got out. Benson parked a half a block away. He waited for her to go inside before walking to the house and entering through the side door that Kyle left unlocked.

The rain began to pour as Bennie parked around the corner. "My kind of weather to do dirt in," he said to himself while screwing the silencer on his gun. He pulled the hood over his head before exiting the car and went down an alley to find a way inside the house from the back.

Inside, Rayvin was going through every room making sure all items were gone. When she finished, she placed the keys inside the lock box on the wall by the fireplace.

"Damn, cuz, never thought I would ever see you step foot in this house," spoke Benson, aiming the gun at her.

When Rayvin turned, he fired the gun. She tried to move and the heels she wore caused her to slip. When she fell to the floor, Benson walked over and stood over her, pointing the gun.

"I thought you was going to be ready. I told you I was going to kill your snake ass for killing my cousins. I can't believe you killed your own brothers." He fired the gun again hitting Rayvin in the shoulder.

"I went to the morgue to see my cousins. They were all riddled with bullets, so I am going to make sure I riddle you with bullets before you die, bitch," he finished, preparing to pull the trigger again.

Bennie came in just in time and fired several times killing Benson. He hurried over to Rayvin who held her shoulder while wincing in pain.

"Come on, we have to get out of here before the police come. I am sure someone heard the shots from his gun," said Bennie, picking up the casings from the gun that Benson fired.

While Rayvin headed to the car, Bennie staged the scene to look like a drug deal gone bad. He scatted some cocaine on the floor and turned Benson's pockets inside and took his gun. He hurried out the house and got inside the car with Rayvin and drove to the projects. The rain was still pouring as Bennie maneuvered through the traffic. When he made it to the projects, he instructed Rayvin to get out the car and lay on the sidewalk. He then dropped the two shell casings out the car window before firing Benson's gun two more times and speeding away. He parked a block away and got out the car and watched a woman come out to help Rayvin. When the paramedics arrived, Bennie went to May's house and waited for his people at the hospital to give him an update on Rayvin.

At home, Kyle sat waiting on Benson to call and confirm that he killed Rayvin. Growing anxious, he fixed him a drink and turned on the television to see breaking news about another shooting in the projects. As he watched the television he spoke, "Soon, I will be watching the news cover your murder my dear Rayvin."

"Negative," spoke Harris, appearing from the shadows.

When Kyle turned around, he dropped his drink when he saw Harris standing pointing the gun.

"How the fuck you get in here!" yelled Kyle.

"You already know what's up," responded Harris, not wasting any more time.

He fired his gun hitting Kyle between the eyes then again hitting him in the chest. Once Kyle took his last breath, Harris exited the back door of the house, ran down the alley to his car, and drove to May's house. As soon as he entered the house, Bennie was waiting.

"Look, Rayvin in the hospital. That nigga Benson was following her, and I arrived just in time before he killed her. She got hit in the shoulder so she will be fine. I had to set the shit up like a robbery and Rayvin got shot in the projects. Man, if I wasn't there, Rayvin would have been gone man, she didn't have her gun on her or nothing. So did you handle that nigga, Kyle?"

"Yeah, I handled that nigga. He will be rotting until someone finds him," responded Harris, pacing the floor.

"Oh, yeah, my eyes in the sky also found the bank account that Twyla was stashing your money in. It's frozen and the funds will be back in our hands in a few weeks," said Bennie.

"You should have let her have that money. She deserves that since I was responsible for her mother's death," said Harris.

"Nah, nigga, fuck that shit! If that bitch needed compensation, she should have come to us and pleaded her case, and we could pay that. Remember Cameron wanted the money, and she wanted you dead," said Bennie.

"That's true! But she had the right to try and kill me," said Harris.

"Anyway! Your mother called me and told me you were planning to meet up with Kevin?" questioned Bennie.

"Yep, I want to hear from his mouth why he left me hanging."

"Nephew, good luck with that! He was around you all your life and acted like he was not your father. Man, I just could not imagine doing that to Lil Ben. In fact, let me call my son because I can't go a day without talking to him," said Bennie.

"You told me about my father so I can start healing, and this is a part of the process. I need to speak with him," responded Harris.

"I get it, but don't get your hopes up. And be careful with my sister, this shit is going to make her spiral. So, when is this meeting going to happen? I want to get back to Florida the moment Rayvin is released from the hospital."

"He is going to text me the time and place," said Harris, going into the kitchen to pour himself a drink.

He selected one of the bottles of red wine and opened it just as his phone vibrated. When he looked, it was Kevin saying he wanted to meet at midnight in the projects. Harris texted 'okay' and poured his glass of wine before joining Bennie in the living room.

June and Rufus

"I am sorry, June, but I love Kyle and want to be with him," said Rufus.

"That's fine, just pack your shit and get the fuck out of here!" yelled June, going to the kitchen to pour herself a drink.

"Fuck it, I am tired of living this lie anyway. We were only doing it for our parents, and May is now dead so what's the point in pretending," said Rufus, heading upstairs to pack some things.

He had plans to run away with Kyle and live in the open as a couple. He signed his divorce papers and agreed to give June everything, only keeping his separate bank account. He was looking forward to spending the rest of his life happy and not hiding who he was.

When he came from downstairs, June was relaxing in front of the fireplace drinking her wine. Rufus sat his copies of the keys on the table and exited the house without saying goodbye. As he drove in the rain, he thought about how free he felt and was looking forward to celebrating with Kyle. He had enough money in his account to live a comfortable life. When he arrived at Kyle's, he exited the car and hurried to the from door.

He fumbled for his key and unlocked the lock before turning the nob and entering.

"Kyle, I am home for good," said Rufus as he closed the front door behind him.

When Kyle did not answer, he walked through the house checking every room. As he made his way to the den area, he heard the television. He approached the couch from behind. When he looked down, Kyle laid dead, his eyes open staring into nowhere.

"No, baby! Please we are supposed to start a life together," said Rufus, hurrying over to the body. He fell to his knees crying.

Without Kyle his life was over. He had nothing else to live for. After crying for over an hour, he stood to his feet and went over to the bar, grabbing the bottle of Jack Daniels and Kyle's gun from the drawer. He went over to the couch and took a seat. He stared at Kyle's body while drinking straight out the bottle. A couple hours later, he was so drunk he could not see straight. He took the gun and placed it inside of his mouth before pulling the trigger.

Atlanta

Cassandra and Destiny stood on the front porch after ringing the doorbell. Once Daisy opened the door, she gave

Daisy a hug. "Why didn't you tell me what time you would land? Lewis would have come to pick you two up."

"No worries, Destiny and I were okay with riding an uber over," responded Cassandra, admiring Daisy's home.

"Grandma! Destiny!" yelled Jamie, running into the foyer. She gave Cassandra a hug before grabbing Destiny's hand and guiding her to the nursery to see her little brother.

When alone with Daisy, Cassandra spoke, "What's this I hear about a distinctive birthmark on our little baby boy?"

Daisy rolled her eyes. "Yes, he is Harris's son. He already knows and we are all moving on."

"Very good then! Now take me to see my grandson, I have a flight to catch very soon, and Lewis can drop me off," said Cassandra, patting Daisy on the back as she followed her to the nursery.

When they entered, the girls were all sitting on the floor surrounding Malachi who was in the baby swing. Cassandra went to the bathroom and washed her hands before joining the girls to play with the baby.

CHAPTER SEVENTEEN

THE TRUTH

It was time to meet Kevin. Harris grabbed his keys and exited the house quietly. He was being careful not to wake his uncle who was snoring on the living room couch. However, the moment Harris closed the front door Bennie awakened. He looked out the window and observed Harris driving down the driveway. Once the car was out of sight, Bennie called his homie Byrd who was already in the projects. Bennie knew where his nephew was heading because earlier that evening while Harris showered, he went through his phone and read the message from Kevin with the time and location for the meeting.

Bennie grabbed his keys and exited the house heading to the projects. When he was close, he called Byrd who confirmed that he had eyes on both Kevin and Harris.

Bennie ended the call and parked at the bottom of the Charlie Parker Square Townhomes. He walked until he saw Byrd who was behind one of the units out of sight watching Harris and Kevin.

Harris sat on the very wall his uncle sat on when he ruined Kevin's life. He lit his blunt and started smoking his weed while Kevin spoke, "This place holds both good and bad memories. I picked this spot to meet because we are both familiar with this place."

Harris inhaled the weed smoke and exhaled. "Yeah, I heard this wall I am sitting on holds a lot of weight. Tell me why you have been around me all my life and never claimed or even treated me as your son?"

"Harris, there is no excuse to why I did this to you. I was young, dumb, and made a poor decision," responded Kevin.

"Wanting to salvage your relationship with Melba was more important than claiming your son?" questioned Harris.

"During that time, yes it was," answered Kevin.

"When did you realize that you fucked up?" When Kevin could not answer the question, Harris continued, "Did you have real love for my mother or was she just a side piece?"

"I had love for your mother, but I didn't want to be with her. She knew that Melba and I were planning to be together forever, but she wanted to be with me anyway. I was young and she is beautiful, so I took advantage of her weakness. She told me she was on birth control."

"Why didn't you do the DNA test to confirm if I was or not?"

"Because I didn't want you to be my son. I didn't want to lose Melba. That was the mistake I made, and I am owning it. I am sorry, Harris."

"So, seeing me all those years did not tempt you to want to be closer with me?" Kevin's silence made Harris upset. He jumped off the wall and stood within arm's reach of him before speaking, "I know why! Because you are weak just like my uncle told me. That's why Cameron was weak and became envious of me. He tried to kill me, and I wonder now that if we knew we were brothers would things have been different."

"I wonder that to, and I am sorry that I caused you so much pain. I just did not want to be with your mother or have any children with her and that is the truth."

"Well, there is nothing further to discuss. I just wanted to hear it from you and now I know. You didn't love my mother. You didn't want me. Your wife was more important than owning your truth. You are scum, that's why your life has been shit," said Harris.

He turned and began walking away but heard a familiar voice, "You never loved me, Kevin?" questioned Cassandra, stepping out of the darkness. When she was closer, Harris noticed the gun in her hand.

"Cassandra, you knew what it was and did not want to accept it. We were young and having fun. You knew that Melba was going to be my wife," said Kevin.

"Then why did you continue to spend time with me?" Cassandra was now pointing the gun.

"Because of this type of shit! You are pointing a gun to me, your father tried to kill me several times. Your sister and her goons jumped me every chance they got. I was trying to keep you satisfied so that everyone would get off my back," responded Kevin.

"You have no idea what I have went through these past years. My family had to hold me up when I was down. I defended you not getting the DNA test in hopes you would love me and your son!" yelled Cassandra, now pressing the gun to Kevin's chest.

"Sis, don't do it! Let's just go back home and move on," spoke Bennie, now appearing.

"Yeah, momma, he is not worth it. That's why I am not killing him. Let's go home like Uncle Bennie said. I am sorry I brought this up and I will never revisit this situation again," pleaded Harris.

"Sis, come on! The last thing you need is his blood on your hands," begged Bennie.

"Right, look at him, he has become nothing! His family has always struggled. He has received and is still receiving his Karma," said Harris.

"Sorry, it's too late to turn back now. What you just said hurt me Kevin, but it's your truth. I loved you more than anyone and anything. And at the end, you still loved another woman who gave you stipulations, told you not to have a relationship with your son. Just think if we were together, you would have been so successful," said Cassandra.

"What! Be a fucking drug dealer family? I never wanted that life!" yelled Kevin.

Cassandra pulled the trigger twice shooting Kevin in his chest. She stood over him and watched the life leave his body. Behind the garbage can Twyla watched. She gasped before hurrying to the rental car and leaving.

"Come on, sis, let's get out of here," said Bennie, grabbing her arm while Harris went through Kevin's pockets retrieving his cell phone. Everyone hurried to their cars and left Kevin's body for someone to find.

Harris sped to May's house. Once inside, he went through Kevin's phone finding the messages between he and Twyla. When he found out that she was at a hotel in the city, he went to his safe in the bedroom and retrieved two stacks of money. As he drove to the hotel, he thought about what he would do once he saw Twyla face to face. When he arrived, he paid one of the housekeeping staff to open the hotel room door.

When he entered the room, Twyla was in the shower. Her baby laid sleeping peacefully on the bed. Harris took a seat and looked at the baby, pondering on whether he should wait for her to get out the shower or just leave. Making a quick decision, he placed the two stacks of money on the pillow next to the baby and quietly exited the room.

When Twyla exited the bathroom, she found the money laying by the pillow. She opened the hotel door and looked up and down the hallway before closing the door and placing the chain on it. She went to the window and looked down just in time to see Harris walking across the street to his car. Before he entered the car, he turned and looked up staring directly at the window Twyla was standing in. She took a step back hoping he would not see her and be tempted to come back. When she peaked again the car was gone. Relieved, she packed her bags and drove to the airport. She turned in the rental car before purchasing a one-way ticket to Texas paying cash. The next flight would not leave until the next morning, so she stayed at a hotel close to the airport.

As she laid in bed holding her baby, she kept replaying what she witnessed in the projects and Harris standing by his car looking up at her. The fact that he had access to her but did not kill her spoke in volumes. Watching him confront his father made Twyla look at him in a different light. She was angry that he was the cause of her mother dying, but the reality was he was young and misguided. Learning that his mother had the same struggles humbled her rage and Twyla now regretted seeking revenge on him. She hoped that one day she could tell Harris the truth that Cameron Jr. was his son, but she had to make sure that no one would kill her.

Bennie and Cassandra

After tossing the gun into the lake, Bennie, Byrd, and Cassandra headed to drop Byrd off at his house.

"You good, sis?" questioned Bennie, looking in the rearview mirror at Cassandra.

She was staring out the window. She looked up, making eye contact in the mirror. She then briefly nodded before returning her gaze outside the window.

All she could think about was Kevin's words before she killed him. It was his truth; he did not love her. So, she reacted on emotion. Now that Kevin was dead, the small hope she held in her heart that he would be with her at the end was now a void. Now she was consumed with pain and life did not seem to have any quality. She needed to numb herself for a moment so she would not do anything else stupid. When Bennie stopped at the next red light, she hurried out the car and dashed down the street.

"Fuck!" yelled Bennie, putting the car in park.

He jumped out and began chasing his sister. But just like when they were children, he could never catch her. After running for two blocks, Bennie had to stop to catch his breath. Byrd drove down the block and eased alongside of him rolling the window down.

"Come on, cuz, I will get my people on it. We will find her."

Bennie continued to watch his sister run until she was out of his view before getting inside the car.

At May's house, Harris laid in bed staring at the ceiling fan turn slowly while thinking about everything. It felt like the world was crashing down on him and he did not know the first thing to do. He thought about calling Tameka to vent but he decided to wait until he got back home. Harris thought about some of the coping strategies his therapist taught him. He got out of bed and went down to the living room, turned-on meditation music, lit a palo santos before lighting his blunt. After taking a seat on the rug in front of the fireplace he closed his eyes and began thinking about his children. The images of each of them and the funny times made him smile. After several minutes, he could feel his stress decreasing. He inhaled and exhaled once more before opening his eyes.

Feeling much calmer, he continued smoking as he watched the flames in the fireplace. It was 4:00am and he wondered if Rayvin was awake, so he texted her, *I love you.*

The front door opened, and Bennie entered. When Harris looked at his uncle, he could see the stress on his face.

"Where is my mother?" Harris questioned.

Bennie snatched the weed out of his hand before responding, "Probably somewhere smoking crack. She hopped out the car and made a run for it after we tossed the gun in the lake."

"Damn, another problem," said Harris, shaking his head.

"Shit, that's all your meditating ass have to say. I warned you not to open pandora's box. Now my sister running around here tripping. Back in the day when she got like this, I had my sister and mother to help with her. But now it's just me and her and I don't know how this is going to go," spoke Bennie.

"What you mean! I am here and I can help you with her now," responded Harris, feeling offended.

"Nephew, if you had your mother's best interest, you would have taken my warning serious and not confronted her on the phone at the airport. She didn't need to know you were coming here to meet with your father. Talking about simmering retribution! I know this is my karma for giving him that crack back in the day," said Bennie.

"I will drive around and see if I can find her," said Harris, standing up from the rug and going upstairs. He got dressed and grabbed his gun and keys before leaving Bennie who had fallen asleep on the couch.

Harris spent the next three hours driving around all the spots he knew crackheads hung out. When he could not find his mother anywhere, he gave up and went back to May's house to get a couple hours of sleep.

Two Days Later

"Hey, cuz, my people have eyes on Cassandra. She at one of the crack houses on the eastside. Come snatch me up," said Byrd.

"Okay, I am on my way," responded Bennie before ending the call.

He hurried and dressed before leaving. It was 10:00am. He did not bother to text Harris who was at the hospital waiting for Rayvin's discharge to be completed. They were all scheduled to leave Kansas City later tonight. Bennie purchased his sister a plane ticket and prayed that he found her before he had to leave. As he drove, he talked to God for the first time and repented for his sins. When he arrived, Byrd was already outside waiting. He got into the passenger seat and instructed Bennie on where to go.

When they arrived at the Hill Top Townhomes, one of Byrd's homies confirmed that Cassandra was still inside the abandoned unit.

Bennie exited the car and went inside, walking slowly checking every room until he found Cassandra in one of the upstairs bedrooms sitting in the corner high as a kite. Bennie took a seat next to his sister.

"I am sorry you are hurting but you can't let it consume you like momma told you."

Cassandra began crying while speaking, "I remember what momma said and I don't want it to. But Kevin hurt me, and I just needed to numb the pain."

"I could have given you some weed and a few shots, sis. Look, I know what he said hurt but it's time to move on especially now that he is dead. You have me, your nephew, your son, grandchildren and all your daughter in laws." He gave her a playful nudge.

Cassandra chuckled finding his comment amusing about all her daughter in laws. "I know, I just lost sight at that moment."

"You know you are going to have to do some rehab. You want me to take you to Cali or do you want me to find a place in Florida close to me?" questioned Bennie.

"No, I want to go back to California, I love it there. Toni will be graduating next month, and we have plans to live our best lives there. Destiny is adjusting and I don't want to take her off track," responded Cassandra.

"See, you have people depending on you so don't go out like this! We need and love you dearly. Come down to Florida and chill with us until Toni's graduation. I am sure Daisy won't mind keeping Destiny until we go to California," said Bennie, standing up.

He held out his hand and Cassandra took it. She stood to her feet and followed her brother downstairs and out the door. When they came outside, Byrd started clapping before giving Cassandra a hug and guiding her to the car.

At the hospital, Harris went to the parking lot to get the car while the nurse wheeled Rayvin downstairs to the main entrance. While he waited, he texted his uncle Bennie, who did not respond. Once Rayvin came down, Harris exited the car and hurried to her to help her into the passenger seat. When Rayvin was settled, he got back into the driver's seat and drove away. He hurried back to May's house where the personal chef he hired was waiting out front. He wanted to surprise Rayvin with a special dinner because she had been through a lot over the past few weeks.

"Just in time. Let's get you settled in so you can have a real meal. I know that hospital food was bullshit," said Harris, unlocking the front door. After opening the door, he stepped to the side to allow Rayvin and the chef to enter.

"Thanks, Harris, I really appreciate this," said Rayvin, taking a seat on the couch.

Harris showed the chef the kitchen before returning to the living room with bottled water and Rayvin's pain pills.

"I should get shot more often," joked Rayvin before tossing the pills in her mouth and drinking some water.

"Don't play like that!" responded Harris.

"So, tell me what's been going on while I was stuck in the hospital."

Harris plopped down on the couch and was about to start explaining when there was a knock on the front door. He looked at the security monitor and was shocked to see June. "It's June," Harris spoke, heading to the door to open it.

When June entered, she hurried over to Rayvin while speaking, "One of my friends at the hospital told me you were admitted for a gunshot wound. When I heard you were discharged, I was hoping to find you here."

"Ms. June, would you like something to drink?" questioned Harris.

"Yes, some red wine would be nice," June responded before focusing back on Rayvin.

"I was in the projects and a shootout broke out. I caught a stray bullet," lied Rayvin.

Harris returned with the wine and handed it to June before taking a seat. June took a sip of the wine. "Those projects are death traps. Full of animals that don't want to do anything but live off the government."

Rayvin looked at Harris and they laughed before she spoke, "How have you been, June? I know that thing with your husband was a lot to deal with."

"Yes, it was quite a bombshell. But like I explained before, our marriage wasn't built on true love, so I let him go. Then early this morning, I received a visit from a homicide detective. He said that Rufus and his lover your uncle was found dead last night, it looks like a murder-suicide. Now I just don't understand why he explained to me that he wanted to leave and be with Kyle if he was just going to kill him and himself. But I am not going to worry myself with it. It's the one-year anniversary of May's death and I want to spend my time remembering her."

She looked up at Harris and spoke, "Harris, I must be honest with you, I was angry with you about my daughter's death. But this situation has humbled me, and I can't blame it all on you because I also contributed to her shaky foundation by staying in a fake marriage and showing her to stay in a situation that she was not meant to be in."

"You are good with me, June, and I apologize for all the damage I caused. I wish I could turn back time. My condolences to you. Would you please stay here and have dinner with us? I know your new bonus daughter would love to have you," said Harris, looking at Rayvin.

June shrugged. "Sure, dinner sounds great! With both Rufus and May gone, I feel lonely."

"Don't worry, June, we are your family now," said Rayvin.

Harris went into the kitchen and informed the chef to prepare for another person before returning to the living room. He began watching television while Rayvin and June conversated. An hour later, Bennie, Byrd, and Cassandra came in the door. When Harris saw his mother, he hurried over and gave her a long embrace.

"Momma, I love you. I am so sorry," spoke Harris.

"No, son! I am sorry and I love you more," responded Cassandra before looking past him at June on the couch.

Harris saw the questioning look on his mother's face and whispered, "Oh, yeah, June and Rayvin are close now. Rayvin needed a mother and June needed a daughter, so the fit is perfect. She also just lost her husband in a murder-suicide. She is family, let's take it easy on her tonight."

He guided his mother to the couch to take a seat before gesturing for Bennie and Byrd to follow him to the deck to smoke.

"A murder-suicide you say?" questioned Bennie.

"Yep, the neighbor found the bodies last night," responded Harris.

"Man, that's fucked up. You cheat on your beautiful wife on the DL for years, then you leave her and go kill yourself and your lover. That's some lifetime movie shit," said Bennie.

"Don't worry, I am going to bag that ole lady, she is fine as red wine," said Byrd, slapping his hands together. They all three laughed and continued smoking while conversating.

An hour later, the chef served dinner. Everyone sat and ate in silence, enjoying the lamb chops, baked potato, Caesar salad, and homemade macaroni and cheese. When finished, the chef returned with German chocolate cake for dessert.

"This food is amazing. When I come back from Jamaica, I want you to come cook for me and my friends to celebrate my farewell," said June.

"Where are you moving to?" questioned Cassandra.

"To Florida. I want to be closer to Harris Jr.," responded June.

While Bennie and Harris looked at each other, Byrd spoke, "Ms. June, a beautiful woman like yourself should not be traveling to Jamaica alone these days. Would you need a travel buddy?" Everyone laughed but he was serious as he took a drink of his wine.

"Bennie, Rayvin told me that you have your real estate license. Will you be interested in the sale of my house and finding me a nice beachfront home in Florida?" inquired June.

"Oh, yeah, for sure. I am licensed in both Florida and Missouri. You will be my first official client. I know just the neighborhood for you. What's your timeline?" responded Bennie, sliding a business card across to June.

"A month! I will email all my contact information along with giving you the keys before I depart," said June before focusing back on Byrd. "So do you have your passport ready, young man?"

"Yes, ma'am, I stay ready!" responded Byrd.

While everyone laughed, Rayvin questioned, "June, so when are you going to fly out to Jamaica?"

"Oh, honey, it looks like I will be here for another few days so that my plus one can get ready and to test out the merchandise," June responded, looking at Byrd seductively.

"Damn, June! I see you're on your Stella shit," joked Harris.

After finishing up dessert, everyone packed as the chef cleaned up the kitchen. When it was time to leave, everyone got inside Byrd's van including June who was tagging along for the ride. When they made it to the airport, everyone said goodbye to June and Byrd before they drove away. Once inside the terminal, everyone sat quietly waiting to board the plane. Harris stayed close to Rayvin while Bennie and Cassandra sat next to each other talking.

An hour later, everyone boarded and took their seats. Once the plane took off, Harris put his ear pods in and began listening to his R&B playlist while reflecting on all the events that happened over the years.

Harris

I will admit that I am fucked up. I could be a bestselling novel and I would call it *Harris*! Just think about it, a young boy trying to grow into a man and all the destruction he caused. He starts taking accountability and maturing into a real man. My mother was a side chick, and my father didn't want me. My uncle got my father hooked on crack as revenge for rejecting me. I was a master womanizer and kept six women tied up in my bullshit because of my insecurities. Then I fall head over heels with a woman who conspires with my homeboy, who is really my brother, to kill me. I am saved by a major drug family and fall for their niece and get her pregnant. Then I propose to her, and she says no. In the mist of all that, I cause two women to take their life because of my confusion and selfishness. And let's not forget all the children that I have created along the way.

That sums it up pretty much, but I must think about what the message is in all of this. God has spared my life and I am grateful. I need to figure out what my real purpose is. You see, it's about quality of life and I need to figure out what that is. I want love, family, money, and to be successful. I don't want to run the streets and take lives. I want to enjoy the little things, spend more time with my children and watch them grow.

Now I have taken steps in the right direction. But I am still having a lot of setbacks like my mother relapsing, my father's rejection, killing my brother, letting Daisy move on, my oldest son resenting me for his mother's suicide, and my uncle being shot.

However, in the mist of all of this, I have gained my independence and awareness of how important it is to know myself. I would thank Abriella for that because she refused my marriage proposal. She set standards and that was hard for me to accept because I am used to getting my way all the time.

It was silly for me to think I would be able to keep all these women under my finger. I disrespected, manipulated them by filling only the voids of their weaknesses to keep them dependent on me. But overtime these women became my family and I love them enough to let them go so they can flourish and move in their purpose like Daisy did. Now that the smoke has cleared, I have realized my wife has already been with me. She has placed trust in me when I was at my worst, she keeps it real with me even when I don't want to hear it. She has nurtured all my children and continued to love me unconditionally. It's time to man up and get my happy ending.

Atlanta

When the plane landed in Atlanta, Harris and Rayvin said goodbye to Bennie and Cassandra who were heading to Tampa, Florida. Rayvin and Harris would go to Daisy's so that she could see Malachi. Tameka and Karris could leave with them and go down to Florida. When they walked outside the airport, Tameka was parked out front waiting.

"There goes my homie Tameka," said Rayvin, heading to the truck.

Harris smiled as he watched Tameka exit and greet Rayvin with a warm hug. When they were finished, he walked over and wrapped his arms around Tameka before kissing her passionately and speaking, "I missed you so much."

He opened the passenger door and made sure Tameka was inside before closing it. He got into the driver seat and as he drove away. He heard Rayvin in the backseat talking in a low voice, "That's who you are talking about."

Harris briefly made eye contact with her through the rearview mirror before returning his focus on the road.

When they arrived at Daisy's, Tameka and Harris talked in the den while Rayvin and Daisy played with Malachi.

Florida

In Florida, Bennie and Cassandra took an Uber to his house after going to a bar to have a couple drinks.

"Sis, you are going to love it down here, it's really lowkey," said Bennie, dialing Effie's number. When she didn't answer, he called again. When the voicemail picked up a second time, he texted her that he was on the way home.

When the Uber parked in the driveway, Bennie and Cassandra got out with their duffle bags and headed to the front door. When entering the house, it was quiet. Bennie walked through the first level and found Harris Jr. and Lil Ben playing a board game in the den. He questioned why the boys were up so late while giving them hugs and kisses. When they told him that Effie was not feeling well, he left them downstairs with Cassandra and went to check on her. When he reached the second level, he heard coughing from the bedroom. When he entered, he followed the sound to the bathroom where he found Effie over the toilet.

"Baby, are you pregnant again?" questioned Bennie, approaching her. But when he looked in the toilet, he saw nothing but blood. He grabbed the wet facecloth from the sink and kneeled to Effie, wiping her mouth. "Baby, how long have you been like this?"

Effie looked at her husband through bloodshot eyes and answered, "I have Cancer."

CHAPTER EIGHTEEN
THE ENDING OF NEW BEGINNINGS

Everyone arrived at the rehabilitation center for Toni's graduation ceremony. Harris stood out front waiting for Bennie to pull up so that he could assist with helping Effie inside. The Chemo and Radiation were taking a toll on her, but she refused to allow anything to make her miss supporting Toni. When Bennie parked in the handicap spot, he exited the car and hurried over to the passenger side. When he opened the door, Effie got out slowly and adjusted the loose-fitting dashiki with matching headwrap to conceal her weight loss and baldhead.

"Thanks for letting the boys ride with you, we had a rough morning," said Bennie, straightening his matching dashiki.

"Don't mention it! Toni reserved one of the private viewing booths for Effie," said Harris.

They entered the rehabilitation center. Harris escorted Bennie and Effie to the booth before returning to his seat on the front row next to Destiny and the rest of the family. Tameka and Cassandra joined Effie and Bennie in the private booth.

Harris anxiously sat waiting to see the new and improved Toni. He had not seen her since May's funeral. He was proud of her decision to get on track, especially for their daughter. He was also nervous of how the new version of her would accept him. He remembered how he used to abuse her.

Toni seen the monster inside of him and endured his wrath for several years.

The director of the rehabilitation center entered and stood at the podium before introducing the graduates who entered wearing cap and gowns. Everyone stood to their feet while giving applause. Harris held his breath anticipating Toni. When he saw her, they made eye contact and she smiled at Harris for the first time ever.

"Damn, she looks great!" whispered Daisy who was sitting in the row behind Harris.

"She's always looked great. It's just the drugs covered it up," responded Harris.

During the ceremony, Harris could not take his eyes off Toni. When it was over, everyone met at Cassandra and Toni's beach home for dinner so that Effie could be comfortable. June and Byrd, who were still in Jamaica, hired and flew Chef Stew out to California since they would not be able to make the graduation. Everyone relaxed in their own way as they waited for dinner.

Bennie and Harris took an evening walk on the beach to talk about business.

"These treatments are going to kill my pockets. I am about ready to start breaking crack down to sale. Now don't get me wrong, I am not broke but I like to be ahead of the game," said Bennie, lighting his blunt.

"Don't worry! I gotcha. We are picking up from Pax in another couple weeks. Maybe we need to get more and hit another area. Byrd said he had some New York niggas that were looking for a new distributor," said Harris.

"I am down with that but for the next few months, I won't be leaving Effie's side. Hell, if she wasn't stressing so hard about coming here, we would be at home. I had to hire a traveling nurse and that shit cost grip," said Bennie.

Harris stopped walking and placed his hand on Bennie's shoulder. "You do what you need to do and know I have your back. This is what you have been preparing me for. Trust me."

Bennie passed him the blunt and they continued walking.

On the deck, Effie and Tameka sat watching the children play while smoking weed. Inside, Daisy and Rayvin sat in the living room watching the television series Power.

Meanwhile, Toni and Cassandra were in the bedroom having a heart to heart.

"Toni, I am so proud of you! You see how proud everyone is for you! Especially Destiny and Harris," spoke Cassandra, packing her bag.

"Yes, I am overjoyed. But what about you, Cassandra? I heard you had a hard time in Kansas City," responded Toni.

"I had a moment with Harris's father. Like I told you before, that was a sensitive spot for me. But now he is dead and the hope that we would be together is now void. I needed to numb the pain and instantly started craving crack, so I got high. But the moment I smoked that shit, all I started feeling was guilt for doing it," said Cassandra.

"I am personally taking you to the rehab to check in later tonight, but I have a surprise for you before we go," said Toni.

"Surprise! Come on with it!" responded Cassandra, now zipping up her bag.

"Don't worry. It will be later after dinner, but trust me, you will love it," said Toni before hugging Cassandra and leaving the room.

When dinner was ready everyone enjoyed New York strip steak, macaroni and cheese, salad, and for dessert, cheesecake. Full and satisfied, everyone sat around the table talking. Harris reached into his pocket and retrieved one of the black boxes. He looked at Toni who gave him a gesture to go ahead. He took a deep breath before standing up and addressing everyone.

"Excuse me, could I have everyone's attention. I have something that I want to share with everyone tonight." He turned to Tameka who was sitting next to him and kneeled on one knee before continuing, "Tameka, will you marry me tonight?"

"Yes, I will marry you," responded Tameka.

She dropped her fork and held her hand out. Harris slipped the ring on. He stood up and instructed everyone to follow him onto the beach where Lewis waited with a pastor.

"Come on, best man," said Harris, gesturing for Bennie to step up.

Toni gently bumped Cassandra before whispering, "Surprise."

"Girl, this is the best surprise ever," whispered Cassandra.

Everyone watched Harris and Tameka exchange their unprepared vows. When the Pastor pronounced them as husband and wife, everyone ran to them happy except for Daisy.

Daisy

What the fuck is this shit!

All these years and after all the fucking bullshit and confusion, he picks Tameka? I will admit that I always felt it would be me until he proposed to three different women. So, I decided to finally move on knowing that Harris ass was never going to settle down. Then he flips the script and gives Tameka my proposal.

I was here first! We were childhood sweethearts! I been riding with only him all these years and only bared children with him. He kept me tied up for years and I only fucked with one nigga outside of him. I saw myself at the end of the tunnel having all his heart.

I watched him go through all these different females. I even set my feelings to the side and developed a relationship with a couple of them. My intuition was dead on because out of all the women, Tameka was the one I worried about. She was just as close to Harris's family as I was. She had a hold on Harris and brought out the same nurturing side of him that I did. The other women coming in were not intimidating but I was at least comfortable that Tameka was not getting no more than I was. Yeah, I moved on with Lewis and was willing to hide the fact that Malachi belonged to Harris. But to see Harris take the time to plan a proposal and wedding makes me feel some type of way.

Cassandra

I am so happy! Tameka has always been the one because she always had his heart from day one. Don't get me wrong, I love Toni, Daisy, and Rayvin, but me and my brother always felt that Tameka was the one for him. She loves Harris and his children. She is a strong woman to take in a man's baby with another woman. Harris could have given Karris to Daisy, but he chose Tameka and that speaks in volumes.

Bennie

Check my boy out! He has manned up despite all odds. I feel like a proud father tonight. I knew Tameka was the one, but Harris had to be ready to be that man for her. She is good people and will do anything for him. Even in the dark days, she still never stopped loving him. Sure, she may give him the silent treatment, but she never blasted him or acted a fool, except that one time she popped up over Loretta's house and beat her ass.

Like I always say, it's not how you start but how you finish. Over the past year, this man burned to the grown then rose from the ashes like a phoenix.

You see! That's the Grimes blood pumping through his veins. I took a risk telling him about his weak ass father but at the end, the reality made him fight harder.

Toni

Harris has shown me a side of him that I never seen before. When I told him I wanted to get clean and be a mother to my daughter, I thought he was going to throw me out but instead he supported me on my journey. I look forward to living my new life being a mother to Destiny. When Harris told me what he had planned for Tameka, I was on board to help in any way. But I honestly thought it would be Daisy. I could tell that she was feeling some type of way because she retreated to the guest room. I can't believe all that has happened in such a short time, from Twyla and Cameron trying to kill Harris, to May killing herself, Loretta shooting Bennie, even June and Byrd getting together, and that's not all of it. Rayvin sat with me for hours telling me everything. But at the end of the day, we are all still standing and looking forward to new beginnings and happy endings.

Rayvin

And then there was four, well three because I never considered myself as one of his women. We just had some good sex back in the day and that's all.

Everyone thinks that I am a lesbian and that's cool. But as I get older, watching everyone getting married and having babies is making me want some companionship. Harris was the only man I was ever with and over the years, I was too distracted with this street life to give a nigga any time. But now I have money in the bank and it's time to sit back and think about how to spend it.

I see myself with a man and a couple kids. Stay tuned and watch how I do this family shit.

Goodbye

It was time to go back home so everyone packed, preparing to go to the airport. Pax arranged for a private jet for everyone who was flying back to Florida while Daisy and her family took a regular flight back to Atlanta. Rayvin decided to stick around in California and see if she wanted to settle there. Harris noticed that Daisy was out of sight, so he went to check on her while Lewis and Bennie loaded the transit.

"Daisy, are you okay? Everyone is loading up in the transit," questioned Harris, entering the guestroom. Daisy was at the mirror trying to conceal her tears. "Hey, what's going on?

Everyone is supposed to be happy today." He placed his hand on her shoulder.

Daisy felt his touch and turned around to kiss him, but Harris stopped her.

"No, Daisy, we are not doing this," said Harris.

Daisy was stunned at his response. "How the fuck are you going to marry Tameka and I was waiting for you all these years! I moved on with Lewis because I felt like you were never going to change," said Daisy.

"You mean to tell me that you were willing to hide my son from me so that you could move on and now we are having this conversation?" responded Harris.

"Look, there is still time for you not to do this. You still have to apply for the marriage license and everything," pleaded Daisy.

Harris took a couple steps back, holding his hands up, he was shocked at what Daisy was saying. "Then what! You leave Lewis and we ride off in the fucking sunset, Daisy? Look, I am sorry we did not have our happy ending. But Lewis is the one for you, he loves you. Daisy, you will always be my family but you and I both know it's time to move on and be happy. You may not want to hear this, but I love Tameka and she is my wife now. I want you to accept it like I had to accept Lewis and don't do anything crazy."

"What you mean? Kill myself like Cookie and May! Fuck nah, that ain't me. I have children to live for and I would never leave them like that," said Daisy through gritted teeth. She grabbed her bag and went out the room, leaving Harris alone.

He sat for a few minutes before Bennie entered. "Everything good, nephew?" questioned Bennie.

"Yes, it will be, she just has to accept this like I accepted her move," responded Harris before following his uncle out the room.

Everyone said their goodbyes to Cassandra, Toni, Rayvin, and Destiny before heading to the airport.

Texas

In Houston, Texas, Twyla sat in her car crying. When she arrived in Houston, she went to Cameron's family's house, and they turned her away saying that she was responsible for both Cameron and Kevin's death. Melba told her that she knew her baby did not belong to Cameron because he had the same birthmark as Harris. Twyla spent the next month living in hotels because her credit was too bad to rent a place to live. To make matters worse, Bennie used his connections to make sure she could not work in her medical profession, so she was not able to find a decent job. She tried stripping but had no one she could trust to watch her baby. She knew that Harris would help her if she asked but she did not want to risk him snapping and killing her.

She decided to go to a woman's shelter so that she could get assistance on finding a place to stay. She used her phone to google some local shelters and when she found one less than a mile away, she started her car and headed there. When she parked in front of the building, it began to rain so she grabbed her baby out of the car seat and hurried to the front entrance of the church. She pushed the door buzzer and waited a minute before a young woman opened the door.

"Hi, my name is Shelby, are you in any immediate danger or need medical attention for you or your baby?" questioned Shelby.

When Twyla shook her head, Shelby guided her to an office area. For the next couple hours, they went through the intake process. Twyla lied about her current situation telling Shelby that she snuck away from her abusive boyfriend and was in fear of her life. When finished, Shelby took her to the room she would be living in.

While Twyla showered, Shelby took care of the baby, cleaning him up. As she changed his t-shirt, she noticed a very distinctive birthmark. She made sure the coast was clear before taking a photo of the baby and the birthmark. She sent a photo of the baby to her mother before slipping the phone in her pocket just in time for Twyla to come out of the restroom.

"It's late so I will let you and your precious baby settle in and get some rest. My shift ends in another half hour but there is staff here around the clock. If you need anything, just push the buzzer, or go down to the main office area. Here is my number if you need to reach me for anything. I will see you at breakfast in the morning," finished Shelby before exiting the room.

When the door closed, Twyla plopped down onto the bed and picked her baby up. She looked around the room and began to cry. Her need for revenge had failed her and she was at rock bottom. Her credit was messed up and she didn't know what she was going to do to take care of her baby.

Abriella

The moment Harris and Tameka made it home, they put Karris to bed before showering together and going to sleep.

In the middle of the night, while everyone slept peacefully, Abriella used the spare key she retrieved from under the grill on the deck and entered the house. She left Adonis in the car and took time to walk around quietly checking every room. When she entered the master bedroom and laid eyes on Tameka and Harris cuddled in bed sleeping peacefully, she became envious.

She hurried back out the house and grabbed Adonis who was asleep. She returned to the house and went back to Harris's bedroom and sat the car seat in the middle of the floor before leaving. It wasn't until Adonis awakened over an hour later and started crying that Tameka woke up. When she saw Adonis in the car seat, she tapped Harris before getting out of bed to get the crying baby. When Harris opened his eyes, Tameka was standing alongside the bed holding Adonis. At first, he thought he was still dreaming until Tameka spoke assuring him what he was seeing was real.

Harris sat up and questioned when his son arrived while checking his phone for any missed calls or texts from Abriella.

Tameka saw his confusion. "Baby, I woke up to his cry and saw him in the car seat in the middle of the bedroom."

Harris checked his surveillance footage as Tameka went to check on Karris who was still asleep. He reviewed Abriella retrieving the spare key and entering the back door. She then wandered through the house before going back out the house and returning with the car seat. Harris checked the time on the footage video it was 4:05am. He tried calling Abriella's phone, but it was disconnected so he called Pax who answered on the first ring.

"Hey, Pax, have you spoke with Abriella? She used my spare key to get into my house to leave the baby while I slept. I don't understand why she didn't wake me or something," spoke Harris.

"Oh, she made a decision. We have not seen Abriella in weeks," answered Pax, looking over at Carlita who held her hands over her chest.

"Decision! What are you talking about?" questioned Harris.

"Let's just say you will be Adonis's primary parent moving forward. Please let us know if you need anything from us," said Pax before ending the call.

Harris tossed the cell on the bed. He found Tameka in the nursery changing Adonis. She looked back at Harris who had a perplexed look on his face.

"What's going on? Is everything okay?" Tameka questioned.

Harris stood next to her at the changing table and looked down at his son who was wining because he was hungry. "Everything will be okay. It looks like Abriella has left Adonis with me," said Harris.

Tameka shook her head. It frustrated her that a woman could just leave her baby while she could not have any. She picked Adonis up and gave him to his father. "Now, well, looks like I will be his mother now. I have a daughter and son." She exited the nursery and went downstairs to the kitchen to make Adonis a bottle and start breakfast.

California

After dropping Adonis off at Harris's, Abriella and Adamo went to the courthouse and got married before taking a private jet to California. Abriella was feeling guilty about leaving her son but that changed once she arrived at the mansion she would be living in.

"We are legally married, but I want you to start planning our grand wedding. We will have it here," spoke Adamo once they entered the mansion.

"But only if we can start our honeymoon now," responded Abriella in a seductive voice as she followed him up the winding stairway.

When they entered the suite, Abriella was amazed. She walked around admiring all the expensive beautiful furniture fit for a queen. When she turned around, Adamo was completely naked laying in the bed.

He gestured for her to come over. "Like you said, let's get to the honeymoon. We have babies to make."

Abriella walked over slowly, giving him a strip tease before climbing in the bed. She got on top of his already erect dick. She kissed his chest softly while riding him. Adamo struggled to hold on, but Abriella's pussy still made him cum fast like it did in the past. He flipped her over and fucked her from the back until they both climaxed. They laid holding each other before falling asleep.

Hours later, Abriella awakened to find three men standing around the bed. She sat up, covering her naked body with a sheet while screaming for Adamo who entered. He took a seat in one of the chairs and lit his cigar.

"Adamo! What the fuck is going on here!" yelled Abriella.

Adamo laughed before speaking, "What's going on you ask. You rejected me for years and now you want to come running back because you could not get your way with Harris. You gave him a child without him giving you anything while you made me jump through hoops for years setting all these standards. Did you really think that after all of that, I would want to announce you as my wife? Abriella you are tainted and only good for two things, a good fuck and baring my children. By the way, your father crossed my father years ago and we are coming back for what is rightfully ours and that's your position in the organization. Now that you are legally my wife, Pax will have no choice but to let me run the southeast because you are going to be too busy baring my children and continuing my family legacy."

"You think I am just going to allow you to take something I have worked for all my life! I wanted to marry you and bare your children. I gave up my son to come be with you. Adamo, we can work together," pleaded Abriella.

"No, that's not how it is done in our family. The men handle the business and the woman stay at home with the children and meet our needs. You knew this when we went to that courthouse and eloped."

"My uncle will not hand anything over to you ever because my father told him not to on his death bed!" yelled Abriella.

Adamo stood up. "I thought about that and if he is not willing to do that, then I have a resolution. You see, Pax is running Carlita's business and she is a silent partner. If I get rid of Carlita, then Pax loses his spot."

He walked over and opened the door to the walk-in closet. He entered the empty closet and walked all the way back to a hidden door. He punched in a code and the door opened revealing a small room that consist of a bed, desk, television, toilet, and sink. He instructed the men to put Abriella inside the room before closing the door and locking it. Abriella yelled and beat on the door, but no one could hear because the room was soundproof.

Adamo dismissed the men before checking himself in the mirror. He exited the room and instructed his maid to take his black card and go buy women's clothing to fill the empty walk-in closet for Abriella. He went downstairs to his cigar room where his father Abilo waited. He gave his father a warm hug.

"Father, things are going as planned. I married Abriella and in a couple weeks, we will check and see if she is pregnant."

"What about the money?" questioned Abilo.

"I will take Abriella's place and go to Pax. If he refuses, I will kill Carlita, and he will lose his throne. As for Abriella, once she has produced several children, I will kill her," responded Adamo.

"Excellent! But be careful, Carlita and Pax are dangerous. When do you plan on meeting with them so I can hire extra men?" questioned Abilo.

"In another week," answered Adamo.

"I bet Blanca is turning over in his grave! And I look forward to the grandchildren, Abriella comes from good stock.

Maybe instead of killing her, we can sale her. I have a few people overseas that would love a beautiful woman like that," said Abilo before laughing.

Texas

Shelby sat in her office looking at the picture of Twyla's baby. Cassandra had not replied to the texted photo, so she tried calling her, but the phone went straight to voicemail. Remembering she had some old baby photos of Harris, she grabbed her purse and told her father she was taking her lunch. She hurried home and went into her storage room to retrieve the photos. When she found the box and opened it, the picture of Harris as a baby was right on top. She compared the picture to the photo in her phone. The resemblance was without question, Twyla's baby belonged to Harris. Shelby dialed her brother's number.

"Hey, Shelby, how are you?" spoke Harris.

"I have been busy with this shelter, but everything has been going great. I called because a woman came into the shelter. Her name is Twyla and she has a baby that looks identical to your baby picture, he even has the birthmark," said Shelby. She sent the photos over to Harris and waited for him to respond.

"Damn, this baby does belong to me. Is everything okay? Why is she in your shelter?" questioned Harris.

"Well, she came in saying that she was in an abusive relationship. Don't tell me you are abusing women," said Shelby.

"Come on now, you know better than that. But all I can say is that it's a lie and our situation is complicated," answered Harris.

"Harris, you have a child in a battered women's shelter. I know one thing and that is you are not a deadbeat father, so are you going to leave her hanging?"

"Aye, slow your roll! Have you ever known me to allow any of my children to suffer?" said Harris.

"I know that something needs to be done. And I hardly know you, remember mother just gave me to my father and didn't give me a time or day," responded Shelby.

"Well take it from me you were lucky to have a father to take you in. Don't get me wrong, Bennie took care of me well. But imagine seeing your mother and she still was not your mother. But back to the real subject, I gave Twyla $20,000.00 cash a month ago and she is not settled in her own place yet?" spoke Harris.

"Oh, wow!" responded Shelby.

"What did she say?" questioned Harris.

"Classic story, the boyfriend abusing and trying to kill her," answered Shelby.

Harris sighed; he didn't want Twyla to be struggling especially with his son.

"Shelby, please keep an eye on her and let me know if she needs anything," said Harris.

"Okay, deal, I will keep an eye on her. And we need to meet up so that I can hear that complicated side of things. I plan to take a week off soon and I can fly up to Kansas City," said Shelby.

"Negative! Kansas City is old news. Uncle Bennie and I are living in Florida and momma is living in California," responded Harris.

"Even better, I was dreading that tricky Midwest weather. The beach would be nice. I will contact you when I am ready to buy my plane tickets."

"How about I do you one better. You are doing a big thing helping me with this situation so I will fly you here and you can stay at my lavish beach home. Everything on me," said Harris.

"You ain't said nothing but a word. I will get in touch with you in a few days so we can get my ticket," said Shelby before ending the call. She tossed the phone in her bag and hurried back to the shelter. She checked the sign-out sheet to find that Twyla was out with the counselor attending a job training class.

Shelby hurried up to Twyla's room and searched around looking for the money Harris was talking about. She was about to give up and leave the room when she noticed a diaper bag sitting in the middle of the table. She opened the bag and found the money.

Shelby left the room and went back to her office to contact her friend Loren who worked for the credit bureau. "Hey, Loren, could you do me a favor and look up this person for me. I am trying to figure out why she can't find a place to stay," said Shelby.

"Girl, I got you. Give me the name, birthday, and social security number if you have it," spoke Loren.

Shelby read the information from the intake form and Loren ran Twyla in the system. She waited patiently for Loren to go over the information for several minutes.

"Damn, girl! This chick's credit is fucked up and her name has been flagged by a bank for fraud. The bank creditor notes say that she deposited some stolen money into a bank account. After the investigation, it was determined to be drug related which explained why she probably lost her job as a nurse. With that drug flag on her record, she can't use her nursing license nor find any place to stay unless she buys her a home cash because her credit is fucked up," spoke Loren.

"Wow, that sums up why she is here then," responded Shelby.

The girls continued to conversate about other things before making plans to meet for dinner later. Shelby filed Twyla's paperwork before going to the nursery to check on Cameron Jr.

She stood over his bed watching him sleep peacefully. She felt bad for Twyla and decided to move her vacation up a week early so she could find out the complicated side of the situation.

At home, Harris sat on the deck watching Tameka play with Karris and Adonis on the beach. The baby he saw on the bed kept running through his mind. He contacted Bennie who had a friend at vital statistics that verified that Twyla had a son named Cameron Jr.

It pissed him off that she named his son after Cameron, but he figured she had plans to tell Cameron he was the father. The situation reminded him of Daisy, and he wondered if she was doing well after her breakdown in California.

Quickly, his thoughts reverted back to Twyla and his son. He had to admit that he had really loved Twyla until he found out she was really seeking revenge. Instead of telling everyone what was going on, he decided to keep the fact that Cameron Jr. was his son under wraps. If God sees fit to reveal it to everyone else, then it would happen.

CHAPTER NINETEEN
MONOPOLY

Daisy was so upset about Harris getting married, she moved her wedding up a week early. She scrabbled around making sure the event space was decorated to perfection. It was well past midnight when she set the alarm and exited the building. She walked to her SUV where Jamie, Clarissa, and Daisha were inside asleep. Daisy called Lewis who was at home with Malachi to let him know she was on the way home.

The wedding was scheduled for the following evening and now that everything was decorated, she could now go home and get some rest. For Daisy, every day she was not married made her feel empty because Harris moved on and she felt the need to match his move. As she drove, his wedding monopolized her mind. A few minutes later, she made it home. After parking in the driveway, she woke the girls up to go inside.

"Ladies, make sure you wrap her hair up and put on your bonnets," instructed Daisy before heading to her bedroom where Lewis and Malachi were in bed asleep.

Daisy showered and put her baby in the basinet before getting in bed. She laid down next to Lewis who did not stir. She stared at the ceiling still thinking about Harris and Tameka's wedding. She felt guilty that she was so envious of their union. She loved Lewis and wanted to spend the rest of her life with him, but Harris had a hold on her heart that was hard to ignore.

She knew at that point it was an addiction. It would take just as much time to completely get over him as she spent over the years loving him. She said a silent prayer asking God to take the envy and hurt out of her heart so she could be happy with her new family before falling into a deep sleep.

Later, Daisy was awakened by Tameka. She sat up looking around the bedroom in confusion.

"Girl, you have a wedding to get ready for," said Tameka, tossing the robe to Daisy.

Instead of questioning things, Daisy put on the robe. She looked over to see if Lewis was still asleep, but he was not in bed. While in the bathroom brushing her teeth, Tameka was in the walk-in closet preparing Daisy's dress.

"This wedding is simple, but very intimate and beautiful. I love how the party team decorated your backyard, and this dress is stunning!" yelled Tameka from the closet.

Daisy looked at the clock on her bathroom wall and it read 10:00am. "Tameka, my wedding is not until this evening at one of Lewis's event spaces," spoke Daisy. She kneeled and spit in the sink. When she came back up, Tameka was standing next to her.

"That bachelorette party Toni and Rayvin hosted for you last night must have you off track! You were so drunk! I am not surprised that you forgot the time and place of your wedding," joked Tameka.

Daisy gave her a questioning look through the mirror while rinsing out her mouth. When finished, she exited the bathroom into her bedroom where Tameka was waiting at the vanity to do her makeup and hair. Even more confused, Daisy decided to continue going with the flow. While Tameka did her hair and makeup, she ranted about the bachelorette party. Daisy sat in silence trying to remember.

Tameka helped Daisy get into her dress. While admiring herself in the mirror, she questioned who were getting the girls ready. Tameka reassured her that Cassandra and Effie had everything under control and things were on schedule.

"Okay, one last thing," said Tameka, revealing a diamond necklace.

"This is beautiful," said Daisy while Tameka fastened the necklace around her neck.

"Your soon-to-be husband wanted to give you one last thing before you are officially his wife," spoke Tameka.

While Daisy continued to admire herself in the mirror, Tameka left the room to check on things and get dressed. An hour later, she returned with a mimosa.

"Okay, things have started and it's time for you to make your entrance. Here, take a drink or two and please don't spill any on your dress," said Tameka.

Daisy guzzled down the drink before following Tameka out the room and down the hall. When they made it to the dining area, they went out the back door where Bennie was on the deck waiting to escort her down the aisle. Tameka gave Destiny the cue and she began playing the violine. Bennie took Daisy's arm and began walking her down the aisle. Daisy tried to focus on the wedding party as everyone watched her walk down the aisle.

Now at the podium, Daisy looked at the pastor. "Daisy, your partner has written something for you."

Daisy turned and almost lost her balance when it was Harris instead of Lewis. She looked out at the guests searching for Lewis but did not see him. She turned back to Harris who was speaking but she could not hear his words. When it was time to exchange rings, Harris turned and retrieved the box from his best man. Daisy looked around Harris to find that the best man was Lewis. Harris slid the ring on her finger.

Daisy was so wrapped up in how beautiful the ring was, she did not realize Harris Jr. was tapping her on the shoulder. When she turned to him, he handed her the ring for his father. Daisy slid the ring on Harris's finger and the Pastor pronounced them husband and wife. They kissed and everyone began cheering. Harris picked up Daisy and carried her up the aisle while everyone threw rice at them.

Awaking from her sleep, Daisy looked over at Lewis who was still asleep. She looked inside the basinet and Malachi was awake looking up at the hanging toys. She picked up her baby and began planting kisses on him while thinking about Harris.

Throughout the day, she thought about the dream as she prepared for her evening wedding. When it was time to head to the event space, Tameka and Harris parked in front of the house to pick up the girls and Malachi. When Daisy came outside to give Tameka the baby, she could not help but to feel awkward. She looked over at Harris who was in the driver seat. He offered a friendly wave before breaking eye contact. She watched them drive away before getting inside Lewis's Corvette and they headed to the event space to get ready.

While the guest arrived and were seated, Harris and Tameka sat patiently, taking care of Adonis and Malachi. Toni and Cassandra made sure the wedding party was in order while Bennie walked around making sure the guests were seated. Effie was in the dressing quarters with Daisy getting some rest before joining everyone.

Rayvin parked in front of the church and turned to her boyfriend Abisai, who sat in the passenger seat.

"You will now get to meet my other family. They will probably react the same way Toni and Cassandra did so just be ready."

"Don't worry, baby, I can handle it," responded Abisai.

He exited the car and walked over to the driver side to open the door for Rayvin. When she stepped out, he admired how her dress caressed her body revealing the curves she used to work hard to conceal.

They entered the building where Bennie greeted them before taking them to their seats. Rayvin felt nervous as she walked down the aisle staring at the back of Harris's head. She needed Abisai to meet the two most important men in her life.

When she made it to the front, she formally introduced Abisai, "This is Abisai, my boyfriend. Abisai, this is Harris and his wife Tameka."

Bennie shook Abisai's hand before complimenting Rayvin on her dress. Harris stood and greeted Abisai with a handshake before hugging Rayvin. He took a step back admiring her attire.

"Wow, you look beautiful. Who would have thought I would ever see you dolled up," spoke Harris.

"Thank you, I have been trying to get in touch with my feminine side," responded Rayvin before taking a seat. Abisai sat on the opposite side of her.

The music started to play, and everyone watched as the Pastor and Lewis walked down the aisle. When they reached the podium, the wedding party began entering. Karris walked down the aisle tossing white rose petals onto the carpet. Then Harris Jr. walked down the aisle with the rings. Next was Lewis's parents and Daisy's mother before the bridesmaids entered. They were Clarissa, Jamie, Destiny, and Daisha. Harris found it odd that Lewis had no groomsmen, and his best man was his father.

When it was time for the bride to enter, Lil Ben came skipping down the aisle yelling, "The bride is coming!"

Everyone stood and watched Daisy entered as the song "Never Want to Live Without you" by Mary J Blige played. The spotlight focused on her as she was escorted down the aisle by Bennie. Daisy never took her eyes off Lewis who stood by the Pastor.

"She is so beautiful," whispered Tameka to Harris. He nodded in agreement.

Once the ceremony started, Harris sat in daze while Lewis and Daisy exchanged their vows. He was truly happy for her. He was also relieved that the wedding was happening after her outburst in California.

"I now pronounce you husband and wife. You may kiss your bride," spoke the Pastor.

Everyone cheered as Daisy and Lewis shared a passionate kiss. After the wedding party made their exit to go take photos, Tameka and Harris went to the restroom to change the babies before going into the reception area.

While waiting for the reception to start, Rayvin and Abisai found a secluded area of the building to be alone. Abisai lifted Rayvin against the wall as she unbuckled his belt and opened his pants. He entered her and began pounding her pussy while holding her against the wall. Ever since they met over a month ago on a beach in California, they were inseparable. It was love at first sight and things were moving fast. Rayvin moaned as Abisai stroked her until they both exploded. They hurried and fixed their clothing before going to the reception area to take their seats. When Daisy and Lewis entered, everyone cheered as they made their eventful entrance with the wedding party.

Florida

In Florida, Adamo parked in front of Carlita and Pax's beach home and exited the car. He walked up onto the front porch where Carlita greeted him, "Oh! Hey, Adamo, we were not expecting you."

"I apologize for my unexpected visit. However, I need to speak with Pax regarding some things," said Adamo.

"How is Abriella doing? She is not taking my calls. Tell her I am not mad at her about leaving Adonis with his father, I just want to hear her voice and wish her well," said Carlita, gesturing for Adamo to come inside.

She led him to Pax's office where he sat enjoying a cigar and drink. When Adamo entered, Pax stood up and greeted him with a hug before pouring him a drink.

"To what do I owe this visit?" questioned Pax.

Once Carlita was gone, Adamo spoke, "I talked with Abriella, and she wants me to take over things while she is focused on having our children."

"I see, but what concerns me is why she has not contacted me herself," said Pax.

"Well, she feels ashamed about Adonis and is not ready to face you or Carlita," responded Adamo.

"I can see that, but she knows personal feelings have nothing to do with business because the show must go on. Why would you need her position when you have your own?" questioned Pax.

"Pax, you know that the ultimate dream for anyone in this game is to have a monopoly. Trust me, as much as I would love to have one, I simply just want to take the burden of business away from my wife for a while so that she can focus on growing our family," responded Adamo.

Pax called for Carlita to come back to his office and join the meeting. Her decision to allow Adamo to take over Abriella's role in the organization was important. She entered and took a seat next to Pax on the couch and the meeting continued.

"Carlita, Adamo has informed me that he and Abriella are married, and he wants to take over Abriella's role while she focuses on expanding their family," spoke Pax.

"Married! I don't recall being invited to a wedding. Besides, we already anticipated a replacement until Abriella gets back in and that will be Harris," said Carlita.

Her words made Adamo angry, but he concealed his emotions as he spoke, "With all due respect, Carlita. Abriella is my wife, and I don't agree with some random man that you two have not known very long running things."

"Adamo, you know that my brother, God rest his soul, instructed me to never allow you nor your father to operate in such a high rank of the business. So, with that being said, I will be honoring his wishes until I take my last breath. Tell me, is this why you married my niece?" spoke Carlita.

Adamo looked at Pax who continued to enjoy his cigar. He stood to his feet before speaking, "You know what, let me get Abriella on the phone right now. I ensure you that she wants me to take care of things."

He reached in his jacket appearing to retrieve his cell but instead took to his guns and pointed them to Carlita and Pax. Before they could make a move, he fired shots several killing the couple. He exited the beach home leaving the door ajar. He drove around for several hours thinking about what he had just done. He had developed a relationship with Pax and Carlita over the years, but he had to do what was right by his father.

In California, Abriella vomited inside the toilet before sitting on the floor crying. Adamo made her take a pregnancy test two weeks after locking her into the room and it was positive. She hoped that when she was farther along, he would allow her outside the room. Her thoughts were disturbed by a tray sliding inside an opening in the middle of the door. Hungry, she crawled over to the tray and stood up. She took the tray over to the table and sat down before tearing into the street tacos.

As she ate, she thought about Pax, Carlita, and Adonis. She regretted falling for Adamo and wished she would have accepted Harris's proposal. She finished her food before taking the prenatal vitamin that was on the tray. She drunk the remaining bottled water before laying down. She cried herself to sleep.

Back in Atlanta, everyone continued to enjoy themselves at the reception. When it was time for people to share words to the couple, Harris was the first person to grab the mic.

Daisy's heart pounded as she watched him walk to the front to speak.

"This is a wonderful day! Lewis, I want to commend you for stepping up and giving Daisy the man she deserves. I am content with knowing that my children are in good hands, and I look forward to taking couple trips together. To start things off right, I took the liberty of getting you two a gift. Welcome to the family, Lewis."

Harris headed over to the table and handed Lewis an envelope. When he opened it, he found two round trip tickets to Bora Bora.

"When I heard you two were postponing the honeymoon, I did not agree with that because you two deserve to enjoy it now instead of later. And while you two are away, Tameka and I will take care of the children," continued Harris before giving Lewis the microphone and returning to his seat.

While Lewis spoke, Daisy looked at the contents inside the envelop. It made her feel some type of way that Harris gifted her a trip to the place they planned to honeymoon in the past. Harris sat at the table hoping the gift would break their tension.

For the remainder of the night, everyone enjoyed the reception. When it was over, Tameka and Harris loaded the kids inside the car before heading to Daisy's so that the girls could grab their bags and go down to Florida. While in the car waiting for the girls, Tameka and Harris talked about the reception.

"Everything was so nice! But Lewis does not have a lot of family. Have you noticed that we all have very little family? But it's perfect how we all came together and made one," said Tameka.

Harris thought about what she said, and it was true. Everyone had come together due to complicated situations. Now they were one big family, thriving. Harris realized at that moment that he needed the women just as much as he thought they needed him.

While he sat quiet in his thoughts, Tameka spoke again, "Oh, yeah, before the girls get in here. How about Rayvin and her new man. I really thought she was a lesbian."

"Bennie said he saw them sneaking off before the reception and he was sure they went to fuck," said Harris before laughing.

"Well, shit she probably hasn't fucked anyone since you took her virginity! She definitely getting it in to make up for it," joked Tameka.

"Definitely! If she is getting it in like that, there will be some little Rayvin's running around very soon," said Harris.

A few minutes later, the girls came out with their bags and got inside. Harris started the SUV and drove away.

CHAPTER TWENTY
HEIR

When Rayvin made it back to California, she and Abisai stopped at a local convenience store to buy a pregnancy test. Rayvin had officially missed her period and was curious on whether she was pregnant or not. Eager, instead of waiting to get home, she went into the customer restroom in the store and took the test while Abisai stood outside the door waiting. The five minutes felt like five hours. When Rayvin opened the door, she held her hand out with the pregnancy test displaying the positive results. Happy, Abisai pushed the door open and hugged Rayvin.

They exited the store. In the car, Rayvin gazed out the window thinking about how she was going to be the best mother. She wanted to tell everyone but from observing other women, she knew to wait until she was at least out of her first trimester before announcing to everyone.

"I need to call my family, they are going to be so happy," spoke Abisai as he drove.

"Maybe we should go to Jamaica and tell them in person," suggested Rayvin.

"Definitely a better idea! See, that's why you are going to be my wife and the mother of my child," responded Abisai.

"After we see a doctor then we can leave," said Rayvin.

When they arrived at their condo, Abisai hurried out the car and over to the passenger door and helped Rayvin out.

"Come on, baby, no need to treat me delicate yet, I am only like a month pregnant," joked Rayvin.

"You can never be too careful. You know twins and triplets run in my family," said Abisai.

The thought of giving birth to multiple babies at one time frightened Rayvin as she got outside the car. They began walking towards their condo when a black SUV parked. Two men stepped out and called Abisai over.

"Baby, go inside let me handle this," said Abisai.

Rayvin could tell by the serious look on his face the men were not his friends. She walked slowly towards the condo. Once she made it to the door, she was about to put her key in but heard gunshots. Rayvin turned around and witnessed Abisai falling to the ground. One man turned looking at her and pointed his gun, but he was too slow. Rayvin grabbed her gun from her waist and fired killing both men. She hurried over to Abisai who laid on his back coughing up blood.

"Baby, hold on, I got you," cried Rayvin as she cradled his head in her arms.

"I love you, Rayvin, take care of our babies," said Abisai before closing his eyes. He died before the paramedics arrived.

Rayvin was taken into the precinct and questioned on what happened. The police released her for self-defense. Rayvin went back to her condo and went inside. She looked out her bedroom window at the puddle of blood while crying. It began to rain, and she watched Abisai's blood wash away. Exhausted, she fell asleep hoping that when she woke up, it would all be a bad dream.

A week Later

Harris parked in front of Pax and Carlita's house. He took Adonis out of his car seat and headed towards the house. When he stepped onto the porch, he caught a foul odor but assumed it was coming from the ocean out back. Before he stepped into the house, a car parked into the driveway. Harris waited until Aadi stepped out. He stepped onto the porch and greeted Harris and the baby.

"I have been calling Pax and Carlita for several days and no one has answered. I been sitting on the product so I decided to go ahead and drive it up here since I knew today was the day you would come for it," said Aadi.

"Yeah, I called a couple times before I drove over. I figure the recent storms must be causing bad reception," said Harris, noticing the door was ajar.

When he pointed to the door, Aadi pulled out his gun and eased inside. Harris followed with his gun in one hand and holding Adonis in the other. Now inside, the foul odor became familiar as they approached Pax's office. They entered, making the discovery of the bodies.

"Father!" yelled Aadi, running to Pax. Harris held Adonis close to himself while watching Aadi crying. "Harris, take my car and the product and go back home. I will handle this and come see you later." He handed Harris his keys.

Harris switched car keys with Aadi before exiting the house. He retrieved the car seat from the car and went to Aadi's car. When he looked up, Aadi was standing in the door.

"Hey, you sure you are going to be okay here alone? I can take Adonis to this local nanny and come back," said Harris.

"No, just get the drugs out of here, the cops will be crawling all over. I will come down to you after I get this situated," spoke Aadi. He watched Harris drive away before retrieving the surveillance footage and calling the authorities.

Harris sped to Bennie's house. He parked inside the driveway before grabbing Adonis and getting out. Noticing the unfamiliar car, Bennie exited the garage with his gun in hand. When he saw it was Harris and Adonis, he put the gun in his waist.

"Aye, I went to pick up the product from Pax and Carlita. Aadi pulled up right when I arrived. We went inside and found them both dead. Aadi had me take his car and the product. He will be down once he finishes up there," said Harris, grabbing the diaper bag so that he could change Adonis.

"Damn, what the fuck!" said Bennie, heading to the car to retrieve the drugs. He brought the two bags inside and locked them in his hidden safe before joining Harris who was rocking Adonis to sleep.

"Another thing, Aadi called Pax father. He has never done that since I met him. Pax and Carlita never had children," said Harris.

"I could see Aadi being a hidden prodigy. I have heard of some big families keeping their only heir secret to protect them. If I am right about this, I would not be surprised if Abriella was targeted because of her rank whereas in all actuality it's really Aadi," spoke Bennie.

"That makes a lot of sense. Aadi knew a lot and kept close contact with me when I came into the circle. He was the one that showed me the ins and outs," said Harris.

"Exactly! Keep your eyes and ears open, nephew. Let's wait for Aadi so we can see what's up," said Bennie.

While they waited, Harris took Adonis home to Tameka. When he returned, his car was parked out front and Aadi was inside with Bennie who was rolling a fresh blunt. Harris took a seat and waited on Aadi to explain what was going on.

"I looked at the footage after the police cleared the scene. It was Adamo who killed my father and his wife," said Aadi.

"Pax is your father? I thought that he and Carlita didn't have any children," questioned Harris.

"I need to trust you two with the information I am about to reveal."

"If you did not trust us then you would not be here," responded Bennie.

"Good point, forgive me. My father resented his wife for not wanting children, so he cheated on her and conceived me. Abriella's father Blanca took my father's place as head to protect my father who is the true head. We believe that Adamo's father Abilo called the hit on Blanca, so since Adamo had a thing for Abriella, we put her as head.

It was easier for people to think a female would run things because she would not be so intimidating. Only the head of the cartel knows the truth. My father raised me and showed me the ins and outs. He also convinced his wife that I was Blanca's sun. Carlita's position is not because of her brother, it's because my father respected her determination to run the business. Instead of forcing her to be domesticated, he let her live in her truth and the consequence was that they could not have children together," finished Aadi.

"So where is Abriella in all of this?" questioned Harris.

"She decided to run off with Adamo. They had a thing back in the day but her role in the organization was a conflict. Adamo's family does not accept women with other children. I have not heard from Abriella in weeks. Either Adamo has murdered her, or she is locked away. Trust me, she knows nothing about this," said Aadi.

The thought of Abriella being dead made Harris feel sick to his stomach as he continued to listen.

"On the footage, I listened to the conversation between Carlita, my father, and Adamo before he killed them. He wanted to take Abriella's place in the organization and said that she wanted to sit back and focus on a family. Carlita told him no and my father told him that you would be the one that step in her place until she decides to come back. Adamo claimed to be reaching for his cell to call Abriella but instead pulled out two guns and shot them to death. Harris, I need you to step into the role and I will stay in the shadows and continue getting the drugs. You won't lose anything if you stick with me. But you will need to watch your back because Adamo wants your place."

Bennie gave Harris a matter of fact look before speaking, "Go ahead, nephew, but be safe. Byrd and June closed on their house, so I know he will help us out."

"Harris, when you return from distributing this supply, I will introduce you to some important people," spoke Aadi.

"Sounds like a plan! Let me know if you need anything," responded Harris.

"Would you like to stay here for a few days?" offered Bennie.

"No, I need to get back to the hotel and inform some people about Carlita and my father's death and start planning their homegoing. It will be in Mexico. Harris, your presence will be required. You will meet the important people I am referring to," responded Aadi. He stood and Bennie walked him out.

When Bennie returned, Harris was dialing Rayvin's number for the fourth time in two days.

"Hey, have you talked to Rayvin? I have not heard from her since before she left Atlanta," questioned Harris.

"I called her a couple times also. She has not answered or texted me," responded Bennie.

Worried, Harris called Toni and asked if she could go and check on Rayvin.

California

Toni headed over to Rayvin's condo. When she arrived, she used the spare key to go inside. When she entered, everything was at a disarray. Toni walked through slowly while calling Rayvin's name. When she made it to the master bedroom, she found Rayvin in her bed curled up in the fetal position crying.

"Rayvin, what's wrong? Are you okay?" questioned Toni, hurrying over to her.

Feeling weak, Rayvin struggled to pull herself up. She wiped some of her tears before responding, "Abisai and I were coming home a week ago and two guys pulled up and killed him. I shot the two men, and the cops ruled it as self-defense. But Abisai's gone, and I am pregnant! This is not how I wanted to bring a child here."

She laid back down and continued crying. Toni put her purse down and held Rayvin until she fell asleep. Once Rayvin was in a deep sleep, Toni got up and began cleaning up.

A couple hours later, Harris texted her to find out if she contacted Rayvin. Toni checked on Rayvin who was still asleep before exiting and going to her car. While driving to pick up Destiny from school, she talked to Harris.

"Things are not good here. Abisai was murdered a week ago. Rayvin killed the two men and was cleared on self-defense. She has been in her condo depressed. When I arrived, she was crying, and her phone was not charged. And get this, she found out she was pregnant the day that Abisai was killed," finished Toni, parking in front of the school.

"Fuck! If it's not one thing it's another. Shit messed up this way also. Pax and Carlita are dead," said Harris.

"That's not good at all. Don't worry, I am going to handle things down here and keep you posted. I am picking up Destiny right now and we are going over to Rayvin's to have dinner with her. I am going to try and convince her to come stay with us," said Toni before ending the call.

Harris tossed the phone on the table and began rubbing his head. It seemed like every time he took two steps forward, he fell back a full flight of stairs. Bennie observed his nephew for several minutes.

"What's going on?" Bennie inquired.

Harris sighed before responding, "Abisai is dead. Rayvin killed the men who did it. Now she is at her condo depressed and pregnant."

"Nephew, I want you to handle this money business. June and I am going to get Rayvin and bring her here," said Bennie.

"That's a plan. I will have Tameka look after Effie and Lil Ben," said Harris, dialing Tameka's number.

In California, Adamo and his father sat in his cigar room watching news coverage on Pax and Carlita's bodies found in their home.

"Son, you have made me proud. You handled Pax and Carlita without my help. Now I know for sure you are ready to run our empire and take over," said Abilo.

"I have even better news! Abriella is pregnant," said Adamo.

"Finally, our legacy will continue growing. So, what's next with our plan to take over the southeast area?" asked Abilo.

"The services will probably be in another week. But I will attend and see who the connect will be. Whoever it is will stay close to Aadi. I will step in and inform everyone that I will be taking over for Abriella and whomever thought they were taking over will be voided," said Adamo.

"Perfect, your marriage to Abriella will give you say over everything. When will you tell her about her family?" questioned Abilo.

"I don't plan on telling her because I don't want her to stress while carrying my baby," said Adamo.

"That makes sense, you have made me proud, son!" said Abilo.

Adamo finished his drink before standing. "Welp, father, I will be going out with friends tonight to celebrate one of my many victories to come." He exited the cigar room and headed upstairs to get dressed.

At the condo, Rayvin sat at the table staring at the food on her plate. She knew she needed to nourish the baby that was growing inside of her, but the depression made her too weak to pick up the fork.

"Maybe you should come stay with us for a while, Rayvin. We would love to have you," said Toni.

"Yeah, Aunt Rayvin, please come stay with us! It's so boring just sitting at home with momma all day," said Destiny, trying to lighten things up.

Rayvin continued staring at her food thinking about the short-lived relationship. It ran like a movie from the day they first met to the day he was murdered. She could not believe after all the years of being alone that God would give her a taste of true love and then take it away.

The relationship was accelerated. What takes decades to achieve with someone only took a couple of months between Abisai and Rayvin. Now she was blessed with a child that would always remind her of this short-lived love. She wondered why the men killed Abisai but for now it would be more important to focus on having a healthy baby because if she lost it, she would die. Rayvin picked up her fork and took a bite of the steak before attacking the vegetables and rice.

"Have you scheduled a doctor appointment yet?" questioned Toni.

"No, I have been so messed up. I have not thought about it," responded Rayvin.

"Maybe we should go to urgent care to check on things," suggested Toni.

Rayvin agreed before excusing herself from the table. She went to her bedroom to get dressed while Toni and Destiny put the food away. When finished, they headed to the emergency room.

The nurse instructed Rayvin to undress from the waist down and lay down. When the doctor came in, he did an ultrasound. It was early, but he was sure that there were multiple babies. He ordered some labs to make sure her levels were good.

"I can refer you to an OBGYN clinic for your first appointment. By then, we will be able to confirm how many babies you are carrying," said the doctor.

Rayvin took the referral before sitting up. When the doctor left the room, she got dressed and went to the waiting area where Toni and Destiny were playing cards. When Destiny saw Rayvin, she ran and gave her a hug.

They exited the hospital and went to Toni's house. She contacted Abisai's parents, and they were on the way to handle his final arrangements. She planned to let his family know after she delivered and even considered moving over to Jamaica for a while.

In Texas, Shelby and Twyla sat in a local restaurant enjoying dinner and a few drinks.

"Look, I don't normally do this with the women in the shelter, but I feel like you are a real friend," said Shelby before taking another drink of her margarita. She was leaving in a few days to visit Harris but wanted to set a good tone with Twyla so she would start letting her guard down.

"You have been a great friend and I hope this continues after I leave the shelter," responded Twyla.

"You ain't said nothing but a word. Have you heard anything from the credit bureau about the identity theft?" questioned Shelby.

"Nothing yet, I have been disputing everything. But that bank fraud situation is really holding me back from getting a place to live and finding a good job."

"If you don't mind me asking, have you heard anything from your boyfriend?" asked Shelby.

Twyla sat for several seconds formulating a lie before responding, "I got my number changed and I plan to never speak to him again." She took a drink of her water.

"I assume your abuser is the father of your child?" questioned Shelby.

"No, he is not. That's why the abuse originally began," responded Twyla.

"Have you tried to reach out to the baby father for help?"

Twyla sat for several seconds thinking about Harris. She knew he had the resources to help her, but she was afraid to face him. She took a drink of her margarita and looked at Shelby who sat patiently waiting for an answer.

"No, he has no idea he has a son. I am afraid to tell him. What if he reacts crazy and starts abusing me like my ex?" responded Twyla.

"A phone call, letter, email is safe and will let you know where he stands. You never know, he may step up and help you. No pressure though, do whatever you feel. But if I were in your shoes, I would reach out," said Shelby.

The ladies continued to sit and enjoy their dinner. Shelby was relieved that Harris was not the abuser. She needed to see her brother to find out what was really going on.

In Kansas City, Byrd and Harris exited the private plane where the SUV awaited. They loaded the duffle bags from the plane into the trunk before driving away.

"I am glad it's May, I never want to deal with Midwest cold weather again," said Byrd as he rode in the passenger seat.

Harris agreed while focusing on the road heading to May's house. When they arrived, they parked inside the garage and prepared the drugs for distribution. Harris could not stop thinking about Rayvin. He wanted to be with her like she had supported him many times, but he had to keep the business running.

"Okay, we have a couple new people we need to meet with. Let's make it the last stop," said Byrd, grabbing the keys to the SUV.

They spent the next few hours making deliveries. The last drop was in the projects. Harris and Byrd exited the SUV and went into unit 1645. Once inside, they hurried and made the exchange before leaving. Once outside, they were walking to the SUV to leave, when approached by two men. Harris recognized Cameron's brothers Marco and John.

"You down here in the hood like you didn't kill my brother and pops," said Marco. He drew his gun aiming it at Harris.

"Come on, young man, we are just trying to handle our business and be gone," said Byrd.

"This ain't got nothing to do with your old ass! Just walk away," said John, now pointing his gun.

Byrd shook his head before speaking, "Man, these youngsters don't do their homework. Lesson number one, when you draw a gun, you are supposed to be past talking and shoot."

Suddenly, two men appeared and fired at John and Marco killing them. Harris and Byrd hurried to the SUV, got inside, and sped out the parking lot.

While driving Harris spoke, "Damn, I hate that Cameron's younger brothers put themselves in this. I thought they were living in Texas."

"Shit, I don't see why you are surprised. It's not the hard niggas you have to worry about these days. If they were smart, they would have never stepped to us in our hood," said Byrd.

"True, I am just disappointed they put themselves in this situation. I want this shit to be over," said Harris.

"Well, you're not getting what you want! The street shit will never be over if you're in it. We have done too much and have to expect the unexpected," said Byrd.

They made it to May's house to get some rest before their flight back to Florida the next morning. That night, Harris laid in bed restless thinking about the encounter. It bothered him that Cameron's brothers lost their lives.

The next afternoon, Harris arrived home where Shelby was waiting. He was tired and on a tight schedule but needed to talk with his sister. He prepared his luggage for Mexico before joining Shelby on the beach for drinks and conversation.

"She did not blame you for the abuse," said Shelby.

"Exactly, there was no abuse, Shelby. Twyla tried to kill me, and I was rescued from a shallow grave. She conspired with my ex best friend Cameron who I found out is my brother," said Harris.

Shelby was taken aback finding out that Twyla was a stone-cold killer.

"Her credit is fucked up because of Uncle Bennie, it was not my idea," said Harris. He continued to explain to Shelby the root of her wrath and advised his sister to be careful.

The next morning, Harris and Aadi flew to Mexico. Bennie and June were in California with Rayvin. It was the day of Abisai's funeral. June helped Rayvin get ready for the services while Bennie smoked a blunt. When everyone was ready, Bennie, Rayvin, and June exited the condo where Toni, Cassandra, and Destiny were inside the SUV waiting.

The car ride to the church was silent. When they made it, Bennie parked and exited before opening all the doors so that the women could get out. They all walked together inside the church where they were greeted by the funeral home staff, who gave them a program and escorted them to their reserved seats. As Rayvin got closer to the gold metallic coffin, she felt her legs getting weak. She was not prepared to see the love of her life again after watching him take his last breath.

She looked up to the ceiling before staring down at Abisai. He looked peaceful wearing a black suit. His locs were draping down past his shoulders and he wore the ring Rayvin gave him for his birthday.

She was frozen looking at him, the love of her life. She wanted it all to be a dream, hoping he would get up and walk out of the church with her. She began crying as she kneeled, laying her head on his chest. Bennie rubbed her back and Cassandra stroked her hair.

"It's going to be okay, baby, I promise," whispered June.

Rayvin ignored her words and continued to sob. Abisai's body felt cold and stiff, affirming that he was dead. She closed her eyes remembering their last conversation after finding out she was pregnant. She regretted leaving Atlanta early.

"I promise I am going to take care of our baby or babies like you said," spoke Rayvin.

She stood up straight and took one final look at him before turning and walking away to her seat. June sat beside her with tissues in hand while Cassandra, Toni, and Destiny sat on the next row. Bennie exited the church to get some air. He pulled his mask down before lighting a cigarette. While smoking, he pulled out his cell and dialed Harris who answered on the first ring.

Bennie gave him an update on Rayvin as he continued to settle into his suite. Carlita and Pax's funeral service would be held the following day, so Harris planned to spend his time inside the suite relaxing and reading. When Bennie finished smoking, he went back into the church and sat on the other side of Rayvin who was still crying.

Once the services were over, everyone met downstairs to congregate and eat. Rayvin went to the ladies' room to get herself together before going to meet Abisai's family. When she was ready, June and Bennie stood behind her while she introduced herself.

Abisai's grandmother pulled Rayvin down meeting her eyes and cradled her swollen face before telling her that the babies growing inside of her would be okay. Shocked, Rayvin questioned how she knew about the pregnancy, and she replied that she dreamed of multiple fish. Abisai's mother approached her and gave her a hug before placing her hand on her belly.

"Please come back to Jamaica with us. We leave in the morning, we will take good care of you," spoke Abisai's mother.

Rayvin was able to negotiate with Abisai's family that she would move to Florida for the remainder of her pregnancy and would travel there often. Satisfied, Abisai's mother took Rayvin's address in Florida. She made her promise to bring her Abisai's cremains when they were ready. Rayvin knew it was a tactic to make sure she came to Jamaica.

When the repass was over, Rayvin returned to her Condo to make sure the movers packed and was on the way to Florida. She would stay with June and Byrd for a while until Bennie was finished negotiating a house she was buying in June's neighborhood.

Bennie convinced Cassandra to continue her recovery in Florida along with asking Toni to relocate as well. In his eyes, California was too far and not a good place for Rayvin to continue living due to Abisai's death and Harris's beef with Adamo.

At Abilo's estate, Abriella was resting in bed after the doctor checked on her. She was about to fall asleep when someone tapped at the door. When she looked, a piece of paper slid through the slot. She hurried out the bed and retrieved the envelop. When she opened it, there were two obituaries. Abriella cried and she reviewed her aunt and uncle obituaries, noticing they died on the same day. She read a small note enclosed informing her that Adamo was responsible for their deaths.

Abriella flushed the paper down the toilet and continued looking at the programs noticing a picture of Adonis. She missed her family and did not know how she would move on without them. Now it was more important to have more children and continue the family legacy. She thought about Harris and was worried that his life was in danger.

The Following Day

Harris awakened and joined Aadi for breakfast to discuss some things before the funeral services scheduled for later that morning.

"We are going to Ivan's once the services are over so you can meet everyone," said Aadi.

"Is there anything I should expect or know up front?" questioned Harris before taking a bite of his quesadilla.

"I'm glad you asked. Ivan is the head. He is traditional with his ways of handling business. He is not too fond of younger people running things, so you must prove to him that you are wise beyond your age. Martinez, Julio, Lucas, and Emilio are his sons. They make the major decisions with their father. His nephews Lazaro and Arturo handle the drug transactions; you will see those two a lot. And finally, Javier and Manuel are his lifetime friends and hitters. These men are older, but they are very experienced and get shit done. If they come for you, just consider yourself dead. You will see them all later and remember your first impression matters."

"Got you! But do they know that Adamo is the one that murdered Pax and Carlita?" questioned Harris.

"No! They don't entertain what goes on beyond the business unless it affects them directly. Adamo and his father arrived this morning for the services. I would not be surprised if they approach you," answered Aadi.

"Got you, I can handle snakes well. Any word on Abriella?" asked Harris before finishing his orange juice.

"Yes, I found someone on the inside who confirmed that she is alive. Unfortunately, we have not figured out a way to get her out. My current strategy is to replace the staff with people that are on our side and eventually get her out. Adamo has her locked inside of a room that only he and his father can open. Also based on the visits from the doctor, she may be pregnant," responded Aadi.

After finishing breakfast Harris retreated to his room to get ready for the funeral. As he showered and dressed, he thought about Abriella and the predicament she was in. The toxic side of him felt like she asked for it. When finished dressing, he checked himself in the mirror, admiring his all-white attire before heading down to the lobby to meet Aadi who waited.

They got inside the car and headed to the Hermosillo Cathedral where the services were held. Harris sat on the front row next to Aadi who struggled to keep himself together. After the ceremony, everyone went downstairs to congregate.

Aadi assured Harris it would be a brief appearance before heading to Ivan's estate. While Harris stood in the corner of the room waiting for Aadi, he was approached by Adamo.

"You have to be Harris because you are the only black man here," said Adamo, extending his hand.

Harris envisioned himself punching Adamo as he extended his hand.

"As you know, Abriella and I are officially married. She is currently carrying my first child and was too sick to attend," said Adamo.

"Well, congrats! I am happy that Abriella finally has was she wants," responded Harris.

The two men were approached by Abilo. "You must be Harris," he spoke, extending his hand.

Harris shook his hand while responding, "In the flesh."

Noticing that Harris was being ambushed, Aadi headed over. "Hey, Adamo! I didn't see Abriella. Is everything okay with her? Why did she not make it?" he questioned.

"I tried to convince her to come, but the pregnancy has her sick all the time. Now the traumatic deaths of Carlita and Pax really have her so distraught," lied Adamo.

"But don't worry, we have the best private doctors tending to our queen's every need," said Abilo.

"Well, I am relieved she is receiving the best care, but it was a shame that I was not able to see her face. Please send her my love," finished Aadi, gesturing for Harris to come.

"Yes! Send her my love as well. And let her know that Adonis is doing great. He is bonding well with his family," said Harris before walking away.

Adamo and Abilo watched Aadi, and Harris leave. "The fact that he is here in Mexico is a problem. Let's get over to Ivan's and see what's really going on," said Abilo.

When they arrived at Ivan's, Harris was amazed. He exited the car admiring the exterior of the luxury home that hung off the cliff. The view of the Gulf of California was breath taking as he followed Aadi to the massive double doors. Before Aadi could knock, one of Ivan's security staff greeted them and stepped to the side to allow them inside before escorting them to the massive living room where everyone congregated. When Ivan saw Aadi and Harris, he greeted them with open arms.

"Aadi, I am happy to see you despite the circumstances. And this must be Harris," spoke Ivan. He gestured for them to follow him to his office while continuing. "Pax and Carlita were family, and I can't imagine who would do such a thing. And where is Abriella? It seems as if she has fallen off the face of the earth. So, tell me who will be keeping my money flowing?"

Aadi closed the office door before responding, "Harris was personally selected by Pax and Carlita. So, Business will continue as usual."

"Very good! I am glad we don't have to waste any time finding someone to fill the shoes. Since you insist on staying in the shadows, I trust Pax and Carlita's judgement, so let's wait until the rest of the guests arrive and we will announce it," said Ivan.

Satisfied, Aadi and Harris exited the office and joined everyone in the living room while Ivan made a few calls. When they entered the living room, Adamo and Abilo were sitting on one of the white leather sofas having a drink. When Adamo saw Harris and Aadi he stood up and walked over.

"I didn't expect to see the help here. I imagined you two have to hurry back to the states and get the product distributed," said Adamo.

"Let me correct you! Pax and Carlita were more than just my employers, but family and I will be wherever they are celebrated," responded Aadi.

"Oh, I love an enthusiastic worker! I look forward to collaborating with you moving forward. Please understand that I did not mean to offend you. But money does not stop and you two need to get back as soon as possible to get the next drop," said Adamo, his demeanor arrogant.

While Harris and Aadi looked at each other in confusion, Ivan entered requesting everyone's attention.

"I have a very important announcement to make before we can carry on this evening. Since our tragic loss of Pax and Carlita, who we will miss dearly, I have received a lot of questions about who will be taking over the southeast region. So, I am pleased to announce that Harris will be taking over effective immediately," said Ivan, raising his glass.

Aadi observed Adamo looking at his father. Angry, Abilo spoke, "Ivan, with all due respect, how does a Black man from the ghetto become the distributor for the southeast region? No one in this room knows him and my son is married to Abriella, so why not him? He has definitely earned it."

"Adamo! Your father is out of line," said Martinez, walking towards them.

"My son, stop! No need to waste any time or emotion on this. Abilo, you and I come from the same generation, and you know what respect is. Let me remind you that I only entertain the business. I trust Pax and Carlita's judgement and will follow through as I did when Blanca trusted Pax and Carlita. Your outburst has spoiled my mood. So, with that, I would like to thank everyone for coming out. I feel some of you may be emotional and in fear of making a serious mistake, I would like to end this gathering. Harris, I will have you stay so we can discuss some ground rules," finished Ivan before returning to his office.

"Harris, we would like to extend our apologies for that. Especially during this time and in my father's home," spoke Martinez.

"No worries, Abilo had certain expectations for his son that could not be achieved," responded Harris. They watched everyone exit before going into the office to discuss business with Ivan.

CHAPTER TWENTY-ONE
CHESS

Effie

As I look around the table, I have a mixture of feelings. I am overwhelmed with happiness and love for the family that God has placed into my life. But a small part of me still aches for my bloodline.

My mother left when I was very young. She was married to my father and when he died, she didn't want to be a single parent, so she just left us with my elderly uncle. My two older sisters helped my uncle take care of me and my two younger brothers. When I turned five, we were placed in foster care after my uncle passed away peacefully in his sleep.

Fortunately, the social worker found a home that could accommodate all of us. I used to think foster care was a good thing. That you would be with a perfect family that was rich. They would take care of you, and you live happily ever after.

But I learned that was not the case. We were placed with a newly divorced mother that lived in the projects and it was always a struggle. Then, one day I met Loretta. She saved me from an ass whooping in the bathroom and she never let me forget that.

We played outside every day having fun enjoying each other's company. We both had issues at home but when we were together, we forgot about all of that.

A couple years later, my foster mother adopted all of us and we moved out the projects into a big house. At first, I was sad because I did not want to move from the projects. But when Loretta's mother moved with her boyfriend a block away, I was fine.

So, every day was full of fun and happiness again. But as we got older things started to change in my household.

Sexual abuse became a normal thing. The people that were supposed to be family began coming around preying on the girls. Nothing was ever done about it. Everyone functioned as if it was normal except for me. But being under aged, I just numbed myself and looked forward to the day I turned eighteen so I could leave.

I remember when I made the big break. It was midnight October 25 on my eighteenth birthday. I walked out of that house and never looked back. I was sad about leaving my younger brothers, but they were fine and had conformed to their new environment while my older sisters moved on with their lives leaving me. As time passed, the bond with my biological siblings dwindled away.

I felt lonely but Loretta was always there, so I gravitated towards her family. I found a job, apartment, and lived the party life tagging along with Loretta on her wild adventures to find the perfect sugar daddy.

Then years later, I met Bennie.

Now we are not perfect, but we genuinely love each other beyond the complicated lifestyle we live. I don't have to worry about my son being abused and we have each other's back through the worse things. Sometimes I wonder about my siblings but at the end of the day, if it's in God's plan for me to reunite with them then it would happen.

When the chef entered the dining area, everyone cheered while he and his staff placed the various dishes in the center of the table.

"Yes! I'm so hungry," said Rayvin, rubbing her big belly.

"Those triplets you are carrying keep you in the refrigerator," joked Bennie, standing up from his seat.

Bennie led grace before sitting down to enjoy the lambchops, stuffed lobster, steak, fried chicken, and various other side dishes. It was so quiet all you could hear was smacking and silverware clanking the plates. Harris looked up from his plate at his family and noticed for the first time in a while they were all together in the same room happy. He was proud of how far everyone had come despite all the drama. From Effie beating cancer to Rayvin pregnant with triplets.

From hustling in the projects to now a major distributor for the cartel for the entire southeast region. He now owned many commercial and residential properties all over the country along with two dispensaries, one in California and the other in Colorado. He was happy that his uncle was able to relax and create the family he deserved. He hoped there would be more days like this and less drama.

California

In California, Abriella laid in the bed trying to relax after her babies fell asleep. She had given birth to her twin sons a few weeks early and they were healthy. Adamo allowed her out the locked room and she was spending her days taking care of the babies and nursing herself back to a healthy place. Aadi constantly sent allies to the estate to work as staff and tried to help Abriella escape. On many occasions, Abriella had the opportunity to get away, but she had to think about her babies first.

Abriella finally fell into a deep sleep but not even an hour later, she was awakened by Adamo on top of her.

"It's time to work on our next pregnancy," spoke Adamo.

He forced her legs open before slipping his erection inside. While he pumped away, Abriella laid numb hoping her babies did not wake up. She slipped her hand under her cover and retrieved the needle with poison inside. As soon as Adamo climaxed, she stuck the needle in his neck. She watched him go into shock before falling off the bed onto the floor and taking his last breath. Abriella grabbed his gun from the nightstand and the second needle of poison. She exited the bedroom and locked the door. She headed straight to Abilo's bedroom and crept inside.

She stood over him with a mischievous smile on her face. Feeling strange, Abilo opened his eyes and saw Abriella before she stuck the needle in his neck. Once he was dead, she exited the suite. It was midnight as she stood at the banister towering over the foyer.

I know you did not think I would just fall into Adamo's trap. You see, he and his father had a plan not realizing that there has been a plan in the making since they killed my father. Let's be clear that Adamo was never my type, I just saw his weak ass as an opportunity. Now I did want marriage and children, but my need for power trumps it all. I hate to say but Harris was a pawn in my plan. When my uncle and aunt put him on, it was truly because they felt he was the one. But as for me, I just wanted to fuck him and use him to wheel Adamo back in.

Abriella

You see, Adonis would have been considered the next to step up, so Adamo knew that the only way he could win was to marry me. Unfortunately, my uncle and aunts' death were not a part of the plan, and I would forever regret what happened.

When I learned that Aadi was the secret, I had to respect his position, but I did not want to lose power. I had to make a move that would secure my place on top of the food chain. So, when he was ready to step up, I would not fall short. Gaining the southwest region was only right so I made sure I married and gave birth to the legacy. I even went as far as naming them Abilo and Adamo. I will raise my boys to be powerful like me.

Word of advice, never underestimate a woman because we hold the key in our womb.

Texas

Twyla and Shelby sat inside the living room playing with Cameron Jr.

Over the past few months, they developed a close relationship. Twyla's credit situation was resolved, and she was able to move out the shelter. She found an apartment not far from Shelby and a job at a local dental office answering phone calls and scheduling appointments. She had plans to buy a house but was not sure where she wanted to live.

"Girl! I am so happy for you. You got that credit thing together and now you are living a normal life," said Shelby.

"Thanks, that means a lot coming from you. Thank you for being my friend. I just can't believe you are a preacher's kid. Like, you drink and have so much fun, yet you help those in need effortlessly," said Twyla.

Shelby laughed before responding, "You are right, PK's are the wildest because we have to grow up so disciplined in the public's eye. So, every chance we can let go, trust me we do."

"If you don't mind me asking, what happened to your mother?" questioned Twyla.

Shelby took a drink. "My mother is from the other side of the tracks. She had a drug addiction and ran the streets. My father loved her but wanted to please his parents. So, when they found out I was born, they took me and raised me as if she was dead. But the thing that bothers me is that she didn't put up a fight to keep me or try to establish a relationship with me."

"Wow, that must be sad. Not having a mother can be devastating. I remember when I found my mother dead, it shattered my world. She was such a great mother at the beginning but then she spiraled out of control over this younger guy and ended up doing drugs. He dumped her and she fell into a deep depression and ended up committing suicide," said Twyla.

"Damn, I am sorry that happened to you. But to be honest, I would have felt better if my mother was dead instead of treating me like a distant relative," said Shelby.

The women sat in silence for several minutes thinking about their mothers. They shared the same feelings of being abandoned. Cameron Jr. began crying, breaking their silence. Twyla took him to the guest room to put him to sleep. When she returned Shelby was on the living room floor passed out in a drunken sleep.

Twyla tossed the throw on her and began straightening up the living room. When she picked up the glasses, Shelby's phone began vibrating. When she noticed that Shelby was not budging, she looked at the caller id. When she saw Harris name, she jumped back almost dropping the glasses. When the phone stopped vibrating, she picked it up and turned it to Shelby's face to unlock it.

Twyla went to the text messages and read the conversations between Shelby and Harris over several months. It made her heart drop to learn that Shelby was watching her and reporting back to Harris on her every move. Now all the bad luck she had been experiencing made sense. Harris was still controlling her world and could strike at any time. Confirming in the text message that Harris knew about Cameron Jr. being his son, she knew he would always be after her, so she had to hide.

After going through the messages, Twyla placed the phone back next to Shelby and hurried upstairs to get her son. She exited the house and secured him in the car seat before getting inside and driving to her apartment. She paced the floor thinking about what she should do. The more she thought about it, the angrier she became. Her wrath was now at its peak, and she saw an opportunity to hurt Harris like he had done her.

An hour later, she went and checked on her son before leaving her apartment. She jogged back to Shelby's house and used the spare key to enter the back door. She went into the living room where Shelby was still asleep, now snoring. Twyla stood over her and pointed the gun. She fired several shots, killing Shelby before going back out the back door, breaking the window and leaving the door open. She jogged back to her apartment and checked on Cameron Jr. who was still asleep. She showered and packed a bag before taking her son and leaving the apartment with no plans to return.

THE END